"Our reputati

He spoke softly, in a monotone. "We're no longer a credible institution. No pastor or church will risk its money on us. Even our own church yesterday—before all the bad publicity—had little interest in helping us. It's over, Magdalene. We have no funds and nowhere to turn." His words pierced her heart with unbelievable pain.

Chandler turned and walked toward the orphanage. His shoulders drooped with the weight of his burden. The closing of the front door echoed the finality of their future.

Magdalene collapsed on the grass, tears cascading down her cheeks and sobs wracking her entire body. What was wrong with her? She rarely cried. Now, it seemed it was all she did. *Father, please help us. Forgive me for my impetuous action. I only wanted to help. . . .*

JERI ODELL is a native of Tucson, Arizona. She has been married over twenty-eight years and is the mother of three wonderful adult children. Jeri holds family dear to her heart, second only to God. This is Jeri's second novel for Heartsong. She's also written four novellas for Tyndale House and articles on family issues for several Christian publications. She is now in the process of writing her first nonfiction book, due out next summer. She thanks God for the privilege of writing for Him. When not writing or reading, she is busy in her church and community. If you'd like, you can e-mail her at jeriodell@juno.com.

HEARTSONG PRESENTS

Books by Jeri Odell
HP413—Remnant of Victory

Hidden Treasures

Jeri Odell

Heartsong Presents

To the Jewish Carpenter, who promises to make something beautiful of my life. Thank You for teaching me that I truly am Your treasure.

To Sandy—a cherished friend. Thank you for all the hours we've spent together on our knees. I count your friendship as a precious gift from God, given at a time when I really needed you.

And always to my family: Dean, Matt, Kelsy, and Adam. You're each a treasure to me worth far more than gold.

A note from the author:

I love to hear from my readers! You may correspond with me by writing:

Jeri Odell
Author Relations
PO Box 719
Uhrichsville, OH 44683

ISBN 1-58660-483-X

HIDDEN TREASURES

All Scripture quotations are taken from the King James Version of the Bible.

All of the characters and events in this book are fictitious. Any resemblance to actual persons, living or dead, or to actual events is purely coincidental.

Cover illustration by Kevin McCain.

. PRINTED IN THE U.S.A.

one

Chandler Alexandre slid his finger under the envelope flap and freed the letter inside. He unfolded the typewritten page and laid the correspondence on his desk. Glancing at the signature scrawled near the bottom, the name Winston Wallace Williams III meant nothing to him, but the title "attorney at law" following the name caused a ball of dread to settle in his stomach. His gaze moved to the top of the letter and he read:

> Dear Mr. Alexandre:
>   This letter is to inform you as of December 1, 1882, the estate of Warren Baxter will no longer contribute funds to the San Francisco Christian Home for Orphans and Foundlings.

Chandler's heart fell. The breath left his body like someone had punched him. He closed his eyes. "Dear God, no! Please don't let this be so," he begged in a coarse whisper. Glancing at the calendar on the wall, he realized that December 1 was barely a week away. He had a dozen orphans to feed, and his funding had just been severed. Warren was their sole benefactor. A groan escaped his lips. In his entire twenty-six years, he couldn't remember ever being so discouraged. He continued reading the letter.

> Upon Mr. Baxter's death, his nephew now controls the funds and has decided to support

other charities. I'm certain you can appreciate
his desire to use the money here in New York,
rather than sending it out west. We do, however,
wish you success in your venture.

Respectfully,
Winston Wallace Williams III,
Attorney at Law

In that bold script, Chandler's very dreams and life purpose were written away. He rested his elbows on his desk, bracing his head in his hands. *Warren, I miss you so much. You would be heartbroken to know of your nephew's actions, heartbroken to know the orphanage will barely survive until the New Year. There is no money.* Questions with no answers flew at Chandler from all directions. The biggest one yet: *What will happen to these precious children I've grown to love?*

He rose and went to the window. Pulling back the curtain, he glanced at the foggy San Francisco sky. From his office on the bottom floor of the large mansion, he could see the Pacific Ocean far off on the horizon. The house wasn't even that old, maybe forty years or so, but it seemed old when compared to the newer, more modern homes in San Francisco—especially the monstrosity his family resided in.

Resting on a grassy knoll, this was the perfect spot for an orphanage. They were far enough from town so the children could run and play, but close enough when needs arose.

Warren Baxter had not only donated the land and funded the orphanage, he'd also introduced Chandler to the Lord. Until his sudden death three months ago, Warren had discipled Chandler for eight years and been more of a father than Chandler's own had been. Now the dream they'd shared—to provide a safe place for children to grow up and know the Lord's love—was about to end. Knowing that made Chandler's heart hurt.

Unfortunately, in a city like San Francisco, adoptions rarely occurred. Most children remained institutionalized until they were old enough to make it on their own. It seemed only on the prairie, where farmers often adopted for cheap labor, did many children find homes. In an odd way, Chandler was glad that was the case. He loved each of the children so much and couldn't imagine a life without them always coming and going. But now they might be going permanently unless he could find another way. He might have to send them to a larger orphanage in another city.

His father could fund this place for years without missing the money. Archard Alexandre—one of San Francisco's wealthiest citizens—owned a shipping company. As the youngest son, Chandler proved to be his father's biggest disappointment. Not only did he profess Christ, he ran the local orphanage instead of carrying on the family tradition as a shipping magnate. Nothing would please his father more than for the orphanage to fail. He'd like Chandler to join him in the family business but, unfortunately, that offer always came with the stipulation of closing the orphanage for good. That was an offer Chandler couldn't accept because he believed God had called him to this ministry.

"I'll keep this place going somehow and without his help," Chandler declared with grim determination.

He watched Miss Fairchild and the children as they came around to the front lawn with croquet mallets in hand. Kneeling next to their littlest orphan, she helped two-year-old Frankie take the first shot. She had a way with the children, letting each of them know how special they were to her. He wouldn't be surprised if each thought he or she was her favorite.

What would happen to Miss Fairchild? The orphanage was her life. What might a spinster do with herself, if not for the children? They brought joy to her sad, pale blue eyes and a smile to her straight mouth. Only in their presence did she seem truly alive.

He continued watching from the window as she patiently helped the younger children hit their croquet balls. She wore her carrot red hair pulled back into a tight bun, exposing a pale face generously covered in freckles. The same ginger-colored dots covered her hands. She appeared very plain and unattractive until she laughed with the children, and then her features softened and her face shone with pleasure.

When she first came to the orphanage three years ago, he'd tried to befriend her. For whatever reason, she'd avoided him. Being around him seemed to make her uncomfortable, so he'd quit trying. Now saddened, he realized he knew nothing about her except they both shared a deep love for the children.

She jumped and clapped when Bobby's ball rolled through the wicket. Chandler noticed she wore her usual faded blue, threadbare cotton daygown. In the three years she'd served here as housemother and teacher, she'd worn the same few gowns. "All in need of replacement by now," he said to himself. He wondered what she did with her small salary. Though it wasn't much, surely she could afford to dress better than she did.

A lump tightened his chest as he glanced over the twelve children he'd grown to love. He prayed for each by name every day. His eyes lingered on eight-year-old Bobby. He and his sister, Sarah, were the first two children to come to the orphanage. Their parents died on the trip from the East.

In many ways, he'd become Bobby's father.

He wandered back to his desk and reread the letter. Falling to his knees, he sought God's guidance. *Father, please help me. Show me what to do.*

෧

"Miss Fairchild, would you come to my office after the children are tucked into bed?" Mr. Alexandre spoke loudly from where he sat at the opposite end of the long dining table, truly the only way to be heard above the laughter, chatter, and the clanging of silverware and dishes.

Magdalene nodded and wondered at his unusual request. Slicing off a bite of pot roast, she studied his drawn features and knew something was amiss. His dark brows were pulled together in concern. *Could I have done something to upset him?* A knot of uncertainty formed in her midsection, making the roast taste like cardboard and difficult to swallow.

"Miss Maggie, what story will you read us tonight?" Sarah asked from her seat at Magdalene's right. The towheaded five-year-old imp stole Magdalene's attention.

"I believe it's Benjamin's choice tonight. We'll have to wait and see what he decides." She smiled at her cherished charges. She adored all of the children, but Sarah held a special place in her heart. She'd played mother to Sarah since the child's second year. In the beginning when there were fewer children, she'd spent more time with each individually. Now she had to divide her attention among the twelve children.

After everyone finished eating, Mr. Alexandre carried his plate to the kitchen. The children followed in orderly fashion. Mr. Alexandre liked the orphanage to run like a well-oiled machine. He believed children flourished in a structured environment. Magdalene brought up the rear of the procession. Though early on she'd thought he overdid the structure, she now realized how right he'd been. All of the children felt safe and loved.

Mrs. Lindsay, the cook and housekeeper, would finish cleanup while they all gathered in the parlor. Their nightly routine remained the same. According to Mr. Alexandre, children also experienced more assurance with schedules. Magdalene had come to realize the sameness provided security for her as well, and she loved their evenings together, repetitive though they were.

First, Mr. Alexandre taught the children a truth from the Bible; then Magdalene read them a story, and Mr. Alexandre returned to his office. After story hour, she helped the younger children bathe and prepare for bed. Three children bathed in the morning and three in the evening, so each child got a bath every other day. Mr. Baxter insisted on this. After all, he hailed from England, where, years ago, Beau Brummel, an English gentleman and expert on hygiene, urged people to bathe daily. In the States, the Saturday night bath replaced the yearly bath, but most people weren't quite used to the daily routine yet.

At precisely eight o'clock, Mr. Alexandre climbed the stairs to the two large, dormitory-type bedrooms. He and Magdalene each took a side of the room and went down the row of beds, tucking in each child, giving a good-night kiss, and whispering a prayer—Magdalene's favorite activity each day. Tonight she attended to the left side of both rooms while Mr. Alexandre took the right, and tomorrow they would trade.

Both she and Mr. Alexandre finished the bedtime routine. Instead of dragging her exhausted body to her small room between the children's sleeping quarters, she followed Mr. Alexandre down the stairs to his office. He'd been very serious tonight during his Bible teaching, telling the children how all things worked for the good of those who love God, even things that didn't seem good to us at first. His words had haunted Magdalene the rest of the evening.

She waited in the doorway while he lit the gaslight. Then he motioned her to a straight-backed wooden chair facing his desk. The sparsely furnished office offered no comfort. "Miss Fairchild," he began as soon as he took the seat behind his desk. A sigh followed her name, and at the seriousness of his tone, the knot of uncertainty rose like bile into Magdalene's throat. "As you're aware, Mr. Baxter died three months ago."

Magdalene nodded, clenching her hands in her lap. Chandler's deep-set midnight blue eyes appeared hooded under his heavy, frowning brow.

"Being the orphanage's benefactor, he assured me that upon his death nothing would change. He believed his brothers understood the importance this place held to him, and he trusted them to continue the work he'd begun. However, that is not to be." His cultured voice cracked with the pain caused by the words he shared.

Her heart ached for this tender man she'd grown to love from afar. He'd earned her admiration by choosing a life of service instead of riches. Respect grew as she observed his tenderness with the children and now, unbeknownst to him, her heart swelled with feelings she kept buried behind a distant, aloof attitude.

He ran his hand through coal black hair he parted on the right and wore flat against his head. His frustrated gesture mussed it up—the first time she'd seen a hair out of place. She longed to straighten the unruly rebel, but instead clenched her hands more tightly together, aghast by her wayward thoughts.

Mr. Alexandre cleared his throat and continued. "We have lost our funding as of next week."

"Surely not! How could anyone as kind as Mr. Baxter have family members who don't care about orphans?" Appalled that she'd blurted out her thoughts, she quickly apologized. "I'm sorry. I shouldn't have said such a thing."

He smiled—barely, but Magdalene recognized the attempt. "Don't apologize, Miss Fairchild, for I've had similar musings."

"Tell me about Mr. Baxter. I never really knew much about him." She'd always wondered how he and Chandler met and became so close.

"Warren's family owned a bank in New York. His two older brothers didn't share his integrity, so they stopped seeing eye to eye on how to run day-to-day operations. He agreed to retire early for a modest monthly income and chose to come west, so he didn't have to hear about his brothers' unscrupulous business dealings. Apparently, they've since retired and his oldest nephew controls the family purse strings.

"Anyway, on his train trip to California, he met two orphans who were traveling to Nebraska to live with an aunt. God used their lives to touch Warren and gave him a burden for orphans. He never married, but he still had a deep love for children.

"I often took my nieces and nephews to the same park Warren frequented. I was only eighteen, so he asked if we were orphans. That was the beginning of many long conversations as I regularly joined him on the park bench while the children played." Chandler had a faraway look, and she knew, in his mind's eye, he was back on that bench with Warren.

"He shared the gospel with me." Chandler's voice cracked with deep emotion. "It was on that very bench I asked Jesus to forgive my sins, come into my heart, and direct my life. I started going to church with him, and we met for dinner on Wednesday nights to share the things God was teaching us, pray, and encourage one another.

"My father practically disowned me when I told him I'd become a Christian. Life in the family business became more and more difficult. As Warren and I prayed about it, God placed the dream of an orphanage in both our hearts.

"Warren worked out the funding by asking his nephew for a small raise in his monthly income. He lived on almost nothing, putting everything he had in the orphanage, and though we had to be wise stewards, we always made ends meet. This was his dream. I thought his brothers and nephew understood that." Chandler shook his head and a look of hopelessness settled on his face, a look Magdalene ached to erase.

"I'll give up my salary!" She'd do whatever was necessary for the children and for him, too, she realized.

He studied her for a time, long enough to make her squirm, as if seeing her for the first time. "A very kind offer. However, I happen to know the pittance I am able to pay you wouldn't feed our brood for a week."

"Though not much, surely it will help a little." She stared down at her lap, feeling foolish for her suggestion.

"Miss Fairchild, I deeply appreciate your offer, but we need a long-term solution." He rubbed the back of his neck.

Magdalene looked him straight in the eye, something she rarely did. "I've saved most of my salary these past years, enough to help us through a month or two, and we can visit churches in the area, asking for their assistance."

He quietly weighed her suggestion. "A possibility, I suppose." Then his face suddenly lit up. "I have a better idea. We'll plan a Christmas ball!" His normal exuberance returned, and rising, he began to pace. "We'll invite everyone off the social register. People are more generous at Christmas than any other time of year. Between the two of us, we can pull this off. Will you help?"

With each word his excitement grew, as did the dread in her stomach. She didn't care for the rich and had no desire to associate with them. From her experience, they were neither generous nor kind. She hesitated to answer, remembering how her family's Nob Hill neighbors turned their backs when hard times hit the Fairchild household.

He returned to his desk chair, eyes aglow. Opening a drawer, he removed some paper. Then, dipping his pen in the ink well, he asked, "What do you say, Miss Fairchild?" He wrote out a list, not even waiting for her reply.

She wondered how to tactfully get out of this job, possessing no desire to plan, execute, or attend a ball and even less desire to be near him. Being in his company only served as a painful reminder of her empty future as a spinster. "Mr. Alexandre," she responded hesitantly.

He stopped writing and waited for her to finish.

"Perhaps you could work on the ball, and I could write to churches, requesting their aid."

"A grand idea! You send letters, but I'll still need your help on this." Walking to his wall calendar, he flipped the page to December. "I can't possibly put this together without you. We have only a few weeks and can't afford to hire anyone." He returned to his desk.

"I'd like you to write the invitations and join Mrs. Lindsay in planning the food. I'll handle all the other details. You and I should serve as the host and hostess, in case any of the guests have questions about the orphanage."

His words stunned her. "I can't—" She'd worked hard to keep distance between them. Drawn to him from the beginning, avoiding conversation and friendship had proved the safest route. Now he expected her to hostess a ball with him!

"I'll borrow a dress for you from one of my sisters. Nadine is large-boned and sturdy. Hers should fit fine."

Large-boned and sturdy? So that was how he viewed her. She bit her lip, praying no tears would fall. At least he didn't consider her invisible, like most men did. None of them had ever noticed her sandwiched between her sisters: the beautiful, intelligent Gabrielle and the witty, charming Isabel.

"How will we afford an extravagance such as this?" She hoped to bring him to his senses.

"Donations," he said with much confidence, as if they'd already been given. "I'll ask the orchestra to donate its time and several butchers and storeowners to donate the food. If everyone does a little, this will work out fine."

He continued writing his plans and Magdalene quietly watched him. Chandler Alexandre—the most handsome man she'd ever met. With his thick, dark hair and midnight blue eyes, he'd turn any girl's head. His charm and breeding only added to his attractiveness. *How will I ever learn contentment as a spinster if I spend time with you? I'm struggling now, but if we become friends. . .*

She'd never let her thoughts travel any further, knowing full well he'd never see her as a woman. She'd noted the way men had admired Gabrielle and later Isabel. No man had ever or would ever fix his gaze on her in such a way. No, all men saw when they looked at her were red hair, freckles, and a large, sturdy frame.

"Mr. Alexandre, may I be excused? Tomorrow is Thanksgiving, and I have to be up early to prepare the children so we can leave for the city." She recited her excuse, longing to escape to her room to pray for a way out of this.

He glanced up. "Certainly, Miss Fairchild. We'll talk again on Friday."

Magdalene nodded. "Thank you for your offer to drop me off at home before you and the children travel up the hill to your family. My father is grateful he doesn't have to make the trek all the way out here to fetch me home for the holiday."

"Glad it worked out."

"It is so kind of your mother to invite the children for Thanksgiving."

Chandler smiled. "I guess she's finally figured out if she wants me home, she'll have to include the whole brood."

Magdalene turned to leave.

"Miss Fairchild, I don't want to alarm the children, so it's best this remains unmentioned in their presence."

"Of course. Good night, then." But she knew no hope existed for a good night, not with this ball before her. Somehow she must find a way to avoid this task. The thought of a social event made her head ache.

When she got to her room, she examined herself in the mirror. Not fat, but definitely curvy and not at all delicate like Gabrielle. Magdalene's father said God built her for hard work and having babies, but spinsters didn't have babies; so at twenty-three, she faced the inevitable: That left only hard work.

Once she removed her hairpins, red-orange tresses fell across her shoulders and down her back to her waist. Her locks curled, kinked, and rarely did what she hoped for, so she always pulled them into a tight knot at the nape of her neck. Gabrielle said she shouldn't wear her hair so severe, but this way she didn't have to fuss, except brushing it one hundred strokes each night.

The thought of closing the orphanage brought tears to her eyes. This place had become her safe haven when she'd left home three years ago to escape the constant reminder of never having a family of her own—a family like her older sister, Gabrielle, had with her husband Nathaniel and their four children.

No man had ever called on her. No man ever would. She didn't plan to be there when men started calling on Isabel. Here, she found a place to pour out her love. Here, she found people who needed her and didn't care if she was beautiful or charming. How could she lose them?

Lord, these children are my life. Please don't take them away from me. And, Lord, please get me out of this ball. I just can't go. . . .

Hadn't she earlier said she'd do anything for the orphanage? Were the children really so important to her if she wouldn't attend one silly function? Magdalene grappled with these questions until well after midnight.

two

Chandler rose from his desk, stretched, and rubbed the back of his neck. It was well after midnight, and his weary eyes ached for sleep. Climbing the stairs, he checked on the children one last time before he turned in. He'd organized his thoughts and had lists for himself and Miss Fairchild to follow. This ball had to be a success—it just had to be.

Miss Fairchild. . . He shook his head; she puzzled him. Leaning over Sarah, he pulled her covers up under her chin. Then he moved on to the boys' room. As he went down the row of sleeping children, he thought of her offer to work without compensation. He smiled, remembering the passion in her eyes and the determination in her voice. She'd give up everything for the children—just as he would.

Bending to cover Frankie, he heard soft crying. Straightening, he strained to listen. Frankie's bed sat at the end of the row closest to Magdalene's door. Muffled sobs came from the other side of the wall. He stood frozen, wondering what to do. In the end, he only tiptoed from the room, knowing the impropriety of knocking upon her door. A part of him longed to offer her comfort, aware the same painful burden broke both their hearts.

Chandler returned to his office and opened the Bible that always rested on the corner of his desk. He knelt and read Matthew 11:28–30 several times. "Lord, I need rest from this heavy burden, as does Miss Fairchild." He prayed for them both, for the children, and the future of the orphanage. Rising, he turned off the gaslight and headed for the kitchen door.

The sight of Magdalene—head down on the table, a cup of milk nearby, and sobs wracking her entire being—stopped him dead in his tracks. She sat up straight, looking in his direction. Moonlight pouring in through the kitchen window revealed her startled expression and her tear-drenched face. She clutched her robe tighter around the neck. Long hair draped around her like a cloak. The sight of her, soft and vulnerable, caught him off guard. Careful not to step any closer, he leaned against the doorjamb for support, not sure what to say. Their gazes locked and neither spoke. His heartbeat quickened.

Finally, Magdalene broke the spell. She averted her eyes toward the window and in a barely audible voice said, "I thought you'd already gone to your cottage for the night." Self-consciously, she touched her hair.

"No." He had an overwhelming urge to go to her, wrap her in his arms, and wipe the tears away. Where had those thoughts come from? This was Miss Fairchild, for heaven's sake—the woman who wanted nothing to do with him, not even friendship. "I heard you crying. . . ." He paused when her gaze returned to his and his heart momentarily stopped beating. The sadness, the fear, the uncertainty in her eyes echoed all the emotions rumbling through him.

"I'm sorry. I didn't mean to bother you." She wiped fresh tears from her cheek.

Swallowing hard, he refocused on the full moon through the opening in the lacy curtains. "You didn't bother me. I'd gone up to check on the children."

"Do you do that every night? I mean, I've heard you occasionally and wondered."

He smiled, feeling silly. Caught in his secret ritual, he nodded. "Just about this time, once I finish the bookwork."

"You work too hard." The compassion and caring in her voice pulled his attention back to her moonlit face. She seemed so different tonight—so feminine.

"I do what needs to be done, just as you do."

"Chan—Mr. Alexandre." She ducked her head, obviously embarrassed by her slip. "What will happen—"

"Don't even entertain those thoughts. We'll find a way. We must."

She nodded.

"No more tears." He hadn't intended to sound so gruff.

"I'm afraid," she whispered. "For them, for myself." Their gazes locked once again. "Even for you."

"I know." Terror gripped his heart as well. "But we mustn't give in to worries. We can't. We just can't. . . ." He moved to leave, glancing at her one more time, wanting to remember the way she looked tonight.

"I'll try not to disappoint you."

"And I shall try not to disappoint you or them. Good night, Miss Fairchild. Try to get some sleep."

He left the orphanage through the kitchen, heading to the caretaker's cottage just a few steps away. The sight of the moon brought new thoughts of Magdalene. His raw emotions from the long day must have somehow gotten tangled and confused, because all sorts of crazy ideas and feelings about her danced through him. Stopping on his cottage porch, he looked up at her window. Tonight marked the first time he'd actually viewed her as an appealing woman, and it scared him almost as much as the loss of funds did.

❧

Exhausted, Magdalene dragged herself from bed. She'd slept little and the puffy bags under her eyes verified the fact as she brushed her hair and stared into the looking glass. As she dressed for the trip home, memories of Chandler standing in the kitchen doorway earlier this morning taunted her. She felt her cheeks heat up. How she'd yearned for the comfort of his arms.

"Stop!" She spoke sternly. "You're a spinster," she reminded the woman in the mirror. "A large-boned, sturdy spinster, at that. No time for silly, girlish musings."

She woke the children, helping the younger ones into their best outfits. Most were tattered and faded, but they were better than the play clothes they normally donned. She took extra time tying ribbons in Sarah's and the other three girls' hair.

The breakfast bell rang and Magdalene shooed the girls down the stairs. The boys had finished their preparations and gone down long ago. They gathered around the table.

"Mr. Alexandre, do I look beautiful?" Sarah twirled before him.

"Very beautiful. All you girls look pretty as queens."

They giggled at his response. How sad, girls of all ages longed for a man's approval—even her. Magdalene bit her lower lip.

"Pwetty as Miss Maggie?" Frankie's innocent question mortified Magdalene. She hated Chandler being reminded how plain she was.

Chandler smiled at her, undaunted.

Magdalene rushed to fill the silence before Chandler responded. "Girls, don't worry about what Mr. Alexandre thinks—or any other man for that matter. As long as you feel pretty, you are." She raised her chin, silently challenging him to dispute her claim. He had the good sense not to. They all took their seats around the table. If only she felt attractive. Truth be known, she ached to hear someone tell her, even if it wasn't true.

After breakfast, Chandler helped her bundle the children up

and get them settled in the old buckboard—their only transportation into town. He helped her into the back so she could keep an eye on their charges. Bobby sat next to Chandler on the creaky, wooden seat.

Magdalene led the children in rounds of "Oh Susannah," "Carry Me Back to Old Virginny," and "Camp Town Races." Then they played the Thankful Game, each naming reasons they had to be thankful. Time passed quickly and before long, Chandler reined the horses to a stop at the bottom of Rincon Hill, where Magdalene's family resided in a small cottage—very different from their once-glorious mansion on Nob Hill.

Chandler lifted Magdalene down from the buckboard. His touch, as always, sent chills down her spine. She avoided glancing into those midnight eyes and attempted to rush away from his presence, only his hold remained firmly about her waist.

"Have a nice Thanksgiving."

"Thank you." She stared at his feet, afraid he might see all her secrets.

He lifted her chin, and his tender eyes sent her heart racing. Leaning toward her, he whispered, "Don't be afraid. Together, we will find a way to keep things going."

She nodded. *Together.* What a sweet sounding word. *Stop! He's talking about saving the orphanage—nothing more!*

He let go of her chin, and Magdalene ran up the hill toward the cottage, not allowing herself a backward glance. Thank the good Lord she had a whole day away from him and a chance at regaining a little composure. Suddenly, he seemed so different—so friendly.

"I'm home," she called out the moment her feet hit the steps to the porch.

Mother and Father rushed to the door and greeted her with

hugs. Isabel came out of the room they'd once shared, appearing very grown up. The front of her carrot red hair was pulled up, and the back hung down in ringlets. Emerald eyes matched the dress she wore. Once, it had belonged to Magdalene, but she'd left it behind, having no need for party dresses.

"Magdalene, you're finally here! I have so much to tell you." Izzy spun around the room for Magdalene to get the full effect of her hair and dress. "Come." She grabbed her hand. "I must fix you up for the occasion."

Magdalene's indignation rose. "What's wrong with the way I look?"

"Nothing." Isabel grinned and her dimples showed themselves. She nearly dragged Magdalene into the bedroom. "Close your eyes. I have a wonderful surprise."

Magdalene stood in the center of the room, eyes closed.

"You may peek now." Isabel's voice sang with pleasure.

Isabel held one of the most beautiful dresses Magdalene had ever seen. She reached out, sliding her hand over the cool burgundy silk, loving the slippery texture. "Izzy, how beautiful."

"I made it," she declared proudly.

"You made this?" Magdalene could hardly believe the words. The dress was so near perfect, she'd assumed Isabel bought it.

"For the Christmas season."

Isabel pulled out another dress of plain blue cotton and held the frock out toward her. "And I made this for you!"

"For me? But why?" Magdalene took the dress from her.

"I wanted you to have something new that wasn't faded for the holidays, and since you like practical, I kept it simple."

Even though what Izzy said was true, she felt disappointed at another reminder of her plain existence. She forced a smile. "Thank you, Izzy." She hugged Isabel, wrinkling the dress in the process.

"Sit down, Madam." Isabel bowed toward the old wooden chair at the dressing table. "I shall fix your hair and prepare you to wear such a fine garment."

Magdalene followed orders, deciding, just for today, primping would be fun. Maybe she'd even end up feeling beautiful.

Isabel chattered as she worked with Magdalene's hair to put it in a looser, softer style. Patiently she wet each strand and made ringlets around her finger to frame her sister's face. "Quite a few young men have asked Father to court me, but there's only one man I hope asks, and he has yet to figure out I'm alive. But after today, he shall know."

Magdalene listened unenthusiastically. Envy crept into her heart. Isabel had her choice of many, yet Magdalene didn't have a choice of even one. *God, help me to be happy for her. Help me not to yearn for what she has.*

"Magdalene? Did you even hear me?"

"I'm sorry, Izzy. What did you say?"

"Do you think a man of twenty-six is too old for me? Everyone says I'm mature for seventeen."

"I guess not." Her answer sounded half-hearted at best, but Isabel didn't seem to notice.

"I think I'm in love. I'm certain he's the one for me. Do you believe in love at first sight?"

She thought back to the first time she'd met Chandler Alexandre. She'd certainly been intrigued.

"I don't know—"

"Because Mother says she loved Father long before they met. And I'm certain I love Chandler."

Magdalene's heart plunged to the floor. "Chandler? Chandler who?"

"Your boss, Silly."

Magdalene jumped up from the chair, causing Isabel to pull her hair in the process. "How can you love him? You don't even know him!" How could she go on working with him if her own sister married the man she secretly adored?

"I will after today." Isabel shot her a wait-and-see look.

"What do you mean? How will you meet him today?"

"That's the rest of your surprise. Father ran into Mr. Alexandre, and he invited our family to share in their Thanksgiving feast. They were once good friends before Father left the bank."

Magdalene sat down on the bed, sensing she might faint dead away. "Surely not."

"Aren't you thrilled for me? Don't you want me to be happy?"

Magdalene could scarcely take it all in. "How? How did this happen?"

"I've become friends with his niece, Josephine. She adores her uncle Chandler and talks about him all of the time. I've seen his picture and fallen in love. How can you work beside him everyday and not be in love with him yourself?"

How indeed? "He's not my type." She'd never admit the truth aloud and risk greater humiliation.

"Do you even have a *type?*"

"No, Izzy, I don't," she snapped. "Are you finished with my hair?"

"Almost. Come back over to the chair."

Isabel wore a wounded expression, and Magdalene felt guilty. Anger seethed within toward her sister for falling for the same man. No, truth be known, the anger was at herself for falling for Chandler and with Isabel because she'd be the one to win his heart. Magdalene wouldn't ever win Chandler or any other man, even if Izzy helped spruce her up.

When they arrived at the Alexandre estate near the top of Nob Hill, Magdalene could scarcely take in all the grandeur. Their mansion looked like a castle from the fairy-tale book Mother used to read to her as a child. Somewhere beyond the wrought iron gate there must be a prince—a prince her sister had set her sights on, and Magdalene couldn't even find a frog.

❧

Chandler had given the orphans a tour of the house. He'd just started down the grand staircase when two young women in the foyer caught his eye. The one in the sky blue dress turned slightly. "Magdalene!" He stopped halfway down after nearly losing his footing, and his heart stopped as well. What ailed him? Perhaps seeing her coppery hair in the softer style caught him off guard. Maybe the crisp, unfaded dress that matched her eyes caused his reaction, or possibly the color in her normally pale cheeks was affecting him.

"Mr. Alexandre." She greeted him as one would a stranger. Disappointment filled him. Where had the tender woman he'd glimpsed last night disappeared to?

"Miss Maggie!" The children ran past him down the stairs and hugged her. Her stern expression diminished as she greeted each of them.

The other young woman moved away from the children and smiled up at him. He nodded and grinned back. Her eyelashes fluttered downward to hide her emerald eyes.

"Ah, here he is now." Chandler's mother's voice carried up the stairs.

"And the whole brood." Disapproval laced each of his father's words.

Chandler descended the rest of the stairs and was introduced to the Fairchild family. Everyone but Magdalene appeared happy to be there. Her stoic expression said she'd rather be caught in the Pacific Ocean without a boat. *Why does she dislike me so, and why doesn't she wear her hair like that more often?*

"Izzy!" His niece, Josephine, ran into the room and hugged the younger version of Magdalene. "Uncle Chandler, did you meet my friend, Isabel? You must take her on a walk and show her the grounds." Josephine pulled Chandler toward Isabel, intertwining their arms. "I'd take her myself, but I'm fighting a cold and must stay indoors."

Chandler glanced at Magdalene, who'd suddenly become very interested in inspecting the paintings hanging in the foyer. "Magdalene, would you care to join us?"

"No, thank you. I'd prefer to remain indoors." She barely glanced in his direction.

"Come on, children. I'll show you the grounds as well." He didn't miss Isabel's disappointment at his invitation to the orphans, but she continued to hang on to his arm.

"Doesn't your sister like the outdoors?" he asked once they were outside.

"I think it's you my sister doesn't like." Isabel spoke matter-of-factly, and he had to agree.

"Why, Miss Fairchild?" He opened the garden gate, leading them inside.

"Please, call me Isabel." She batted her thick, auburn lashes that fringed large green eyes. "All my friends do."

"All right, Isabel. Why does your sister dislike me so?"

She stopped to smell a pale pink rose. "You're not her type."

"And what kind of beaus does she prefer?" He picked the prettiest blossom and handed it to Isabel. She drew the flower to her nose and breathed in the sweet scent.

"I have no idea. She's never had a beau."

Why did her words bring him both pleasure and sadness? "But you probably don't lack for callers, do you?"

"No, I don't." She peered at him coyly from behind her rose. "But if you'd like to call, Mr. Alexandre, I'd have my father chase all of the others away."

Chandler grinned down at her. *I may need to find a wife soon, and though Magdalene might be a wiser choice, you appear more interested.* "I'll keep your offer in mind." They strolled on through the gardens. Isabel stopped frequently to inhale another fragrance. The children played hide-and-seek behind the rows of flowers and plants.

Lord, if the ball idea doesn't work out, getting married may be my only option. He hated the idea of marrying to obtain his trust fund, but he was running out of options. Magdalene seemed the perfect choice because she adored their little orphans, but could she ever love him? Could he ever cherish her? He'd hoped someday to have a wife who shared his dreams. He'd get to know both Fairchild women better, just in case. . . .

three

Magdalene squirmed, wishing she'd gone outside with Chandler and Isabel. The conversation with the women here in the parlor bored her to distraction. Her mother, Mrs. Alexandre, and some of Chandler's older sisters spoke on fashion, tea, and the theater. None interested her in the least.

She surveyed the large, ostentatious room reflecting the French taste for opulence. The furniture and walls were red damask in the style of Louis XV. Black walnut tables accented the parlor and added to the ornamentation.

Mrs. Alexandre turned to her and asked, "Are you all right, Dear?"

"Yes, I apologize. My mind's on the children. If you'll excuse me, I'll go check on them and see to their well-being."

"Baldwin set up croquet in the Italian gardens. Perhaps you'll find them there."

"Yes, I shall check. Thank you." Magdalene stood and straightened her skirts, liking the feel of the crisp cotton against her palms.

She exited through the front door, taking a deep breath of fresh, brisk San Francisco sea air. The beautiful grounds beckoned her. She followed a cobblestone path to the right and down the hill. Hearing the children's giggles, she increased her gait, anxious to find them. Turning a corner, she ran smack dab into Chandler with Isabel on his arm. The sight of them laughing together nearly undid her.

"There you two are!" She forced a cheerful tone into her voice. "I've come to fetch the children for a game of croquet. Would you care to join us?"

The eager expression on Chandler's face gave her a moment's pause. "I think I'll opt for croquet. What about you, Isabel?"

Isabel got her usual sulky expression when things weren't going as she planned. "I'd much prefer a walk."

"Sorry. I can't pass up a good game. Perhaps later. If you'll excuse me." Chandler pulled his arm free and turned to Magdalene. "Shall we?" He extended his arm to her.

Dumbfounded, she accepted it. They turned back in the direction from which he and Isabel had just come. "What are the children doing?"

"I left them out on the lawn, playing games with my nieces and nephews." His hold on her arm tightened as they trudged down the rocky slope.

"How many do you have?"

"At least a couple of dozen. I've given up keeping track of the exact count because the number changes so often. What about you?"

"Just four."

"Do you hope for children of your own someday?"

Did he know? Did he know how deeply she ached for a family and how much she hurt, knowing the dream would never come to pass? She stumbled over a sharp rock. He steadied her. His face was now mere inches from hers, gaze probing, asking questions she didn't desire to answer.

Feigning brightness she said, "I already have a dozen children. How many more could one woman need?"

Disappointment shone from his eyes. Why would he care if she longed for a family or not?

"Now, let's go find those darling children." She led off down the path.

When the children came into view, Magdalene stopped, enjoying watching the youngsters at play. Chandler halted next to her.

"My sister is charming, don't you think?" She peered up at him, hoping to read his reaction, desiring to know what he truly thought of Isabel.

He didn't even glance at her. "I hadn't noticed." Then he chuckled. "Look at Bobby! He's faster than some of those boys twice his size." The pride in his eyes and voice reflected the pride in her heart.

"You do have a lot of nephews and nieces." All sizes and shapes of children raced across the grass.

"Yes. I'm the only Alexandre with no offspring. My father's none too pleased about that fact, either."

"How do you feel?"

"I have a dozen children I can't feed now. Why would I yearn for more?"

The seriousness of his words brought an ache to her heart. She gently touched his arm. "We'll find a way."

"I've written out the steps we need to take to execute the ball." His gaze roved over her, causing the breath to catch in her throat. "We'll need to begin first thing tomorrow."

The ball! She'd hoped he'd forgotten.

His face lit up. "What if you bring Izzy back with us? She can help."

Not thrilled by the idea, Magdalene said, "Whatever suits you. Maybe she'd even make a better hostess for the ball." Bitterness crept into her words.

"I don't think so. She doesn't love these kids the way you do. You can share your passion and your heart if questions arise." He shoved his hands in his pockets and walked toward the grassy area where the children were starting three-legged races. Magdalene followed.

Most of the children were already tied to a partner, but Bobby bounded toward them, a short piece of rope dangling from his hand. "Will you be my partner, Uncle Chandler?" The orphans referred to him as Uncle because it seemed less formal than Mr. Alexandre. Chandler said he wanted them to have a sense of relationship; he wasn't just the director, he loved them.

"Sure."

Bobby proceeded to tie their legs together. Then they hobbled to the starting line.

When the whistle blew, Chandler and Bobby struggled to find a rhythm. Chandler gave up and lifted Bobby off the ground, racing toward the finish line. All of the others protested.

"You can't win unless you cheat," one of Chandler's nephews objected loudly.

"I can win this race tied to anybody you choose."

"Anybody?" The older boy's interest piqued.

Chandler nodded.

"Her." The boy's stubby index finger pointed directly at Magdalene.

Before she could protest, cheering children surrounded her, pushing her toward Chandler. They tied her ankle to his, ignoring her pleadings.

"We can do this, Magdalene," he shouted above the dull roar. He pulled her close against his side.

Her senses went haywire. *Magdalene.* Twice today he'd called her by her given name, and twice today her heart did a somersault in her chest.

"We'll start with our outside limbs first."

She nodded her agreement.

The whistle blew. Chandler half dragged her as they raced toward the finish line. She heard cheering and jeering, but the sweetest sound of all was Chandler's, "Run, Maggie. Run, my Maggie. Run."

They crossed the finish line at least two steps ahead of their closest contenders. Laughing, he pulled her against him in a hug. "I knew we could win!"

Made breathless by the end of the race, his affection left her more so.

He pulled back from the hug but didn't loosen his hold completely. "We're a great team, Magdalene." Catching sight of his midnight eyes, Magdalene felt weak in the knees. Certain she'd remember those words forever, she filed them away to retrieve and ponder later.

They ran five more races just to prove their win hadn't been an accident. At the ringing of the dinner bell, Chandler led an excited and disheveled group of youngsters into the house to clean up. Afterwards, he directed them to the servants' dining room, where all the children would eat.

"Should I stay and eat with them?" Magdalene asked.

"No, you'll be expected in the banquet hall." He then escorted her there.

Stopping just inside the doorway, she glanced up and whispered, "I've never seen such a high ceiling."

"It's thirty feet," he whispered back. "A fact my father is very proud of. No one has a banquet hall as elegant as ours." Sarcasm dripped from each word.

She agreed, for the room far surpassed any she'd seen to date. A huge table graced the middle of the room. She felt like a small child entering a giant's domain. On the far wall, three fires burned in an ornately carved stone triple fireplace. Tapestries hung from the walls, and numerous red velvet chairs surrounded the table and lined the edge of the room.

"This all makes me long for the simplicity of home. You, me, and twelve little orphans seated around Mrs. Lindsay's pot roast."

"On hard wooden chairs."

"Where spilled food doesn't matter."

Magdalene smiled up at Chandler, feeling the same longing for home. Funny how they both thought of the house—with none of these niceties—as their home. She remembered her father saying, "Home is where the heart is." The orphanage and all who lived within definitely held her heart.

❧

Magdalene had a faraway look, and Chandler wondered what thoughts carried her off. As he studied her, he questioned how he'd missed seeing how extraordinary she was. How, in all honesty, had he missed noticing her at all these past three years?

His father entered the room and took his seat at the head of the table. Chandler helped Magdalene find her place card and discovered she'd been seated at the corner between him and his father. Isabel glared at them from across the table where she sat next to her father. Chandler relished the opportunity to become better acquainted with Magdalene's family but wished they weren't seated so close to his father.

The table filled up quickly as each Alexandre found their appropriate chair. Conversations quieted, and twenty-five pairs of eyes focused on Archard, the family patriarch.

"Fairchild, you're a religious man. Why don't you bless the food?" his father's voice boomed.

Edward Fairchild asked God to bless the food, those who

ate it, and the hands that prepared it.

"And who might these lovely ladies be?" His father's balding head bobbed first toward Magdalene and then Isabel.

"Father, this is Magdalene Fairchild and her sister, Isabel. Magdalene works with me at the orphanage. Magdalene, Isabel, my father, Archard Alexandre." Both girls greeted the short, round man.

After polite responses, they filled their plates. Platters laden with turkey, roast suckling pig, chestnut stuffing, hot rolls, mashed potatoes, giblet gravy, cranberry sauce, squash, turnips, and onions in cream were passed around. Chandler helped himself to some of everything.

When everyone was served, Archard started a conversation. "So, Fairchild, do you and the missus miss this kind of living?"

Appalled by his father's tactlessness, Chandler jumped into the conversation. "Magdalene and I are planning a ball to raise funds for the orphanage." He hated bringing up that particular subject, knowing how his father felt about the place, but he could think of nothing else to say.

"What do you think of this whole orphanage idea, Fairchild?" his father asked before stuffing another bite of turkey into his mouth.

"I'd say there's a definite need for—"

"If you ask me, Chandler could find a better way to spend his time."

Oh, great. Here he goes. Chandler laid down his fork, suddenly losing his appetite. If not for his mother, he would never come back here.

"You've lived in riches and in modesty. Tell the boy, Fairchild, which you'd prefer, given the choice. After all, *he has* the choice."

Edward Fairchild cleared his throat. "With all due respect,

Alexandre, I, too, had the choice and chose a simpler lifestyle when the bank closed. I received offers from other banks, but Jacqueline and I decided we wanted our three girls to have different values than most of their wealthy friends. We walked away with no regrets. Therefore, I respect Chandler for choosing a life of service instead of a life of wealth."

"Oh, hogwash. I should have known better than to ask a religious man for his opinion." He mopped up the rest of his gravy with his roll.

Chandler clearly understood why his father invited the Fairchild family for dinner. He'd planned to solicit Mr. Fairchild's help in opening Chandler's eyes to the stupidity of his ways, but the plan backfired.

"I can only be honest with my opinions. What would happen to the orphans, if not for Chandler and Magdalene?" Mr. Fairchild questioned.

"Chandler should work for me. He'd be a wealthy man and could support many orphans, if that is his fancy."

"They need a father figure to guide them each day. I've told you all this before." Chandler's voice echoed his frustration.

"Then hire one!" His father hit the table with his fist. The whole room quieted, and everyone focused on him.

"You will never understand." Chandler kept his voice low. "Why must we rehash this each time I'm here?"

"We'll rehash it until the day I die, if you must continue to chase foolish dreams." Archard chose a piece of pie off the silver serving tray one of the maids carried.

Chandler bit his lip and held his retort. His father would never understand unless he accepted Christ as his Savior. Money reigned as his god and his motive for everything.

"Sir—" Magdalene surprised him by speaking up. "The

children love your son, and he loves them. What he does is very important."

"And you, young lady, how do you feel about my son? Would you marry a man like him with nothing to offer but a rundown old orphanage and an entire brood of children?"

Magdalene turned twenty shades of red. She licked her lips, took a deep breath, and looked his father square in the face. "If I loved him, he loved me, and God gave His blessing—then, yes. A man doesn't have to be rich to be a good husband. My sister married a fisherman, and he's a wonderful husband and father."

"This is modern thinking. Men are providers; they aren't meant to coddle the women and children."

"Mr. Fairchild, do you enjoy fishing?" Chandler jumped at the chance to change the subject.

"Very much. Out on the sea, a man is free. I never knew such immense pleasure as a banker."

"Ah, now there is something we agree on. The sea. There's nothing like her." Mr. Alexandre's face took on a distant look. "In my younger days, I captained the clippers myself. Now, with a whole fleet to watch over, I rarely get the chance to sail the high seas."

"Can't you understand as much as you love the sea, Chandler loves his life at the orphanage?" Magdalene spoke up again, but Chandler wished she'd left well enough alone.

"From the day he was born, Chandler was his mother's boy." Small brown eyes focused on him—their displeasure evident. "A sickly little thing, he spent more time in bed than out. Thin and pale, he couldn't keep up with his brothers. His mother coddled him, taught him to love art, music, and womanly things. He doesn't know how to be a man." Archard pushed away his half-eaten pumpkin pie. "Now if you'll excuse me." He rose from the table, leaving a quiet group in his wake.

Embarrassed by his father's tirade, Chandler stared at his piece of mincemeat pie, no longer the least bit tempted. What must Magdalene and her family think of him now? The room was suddenly so silent that he heard Magdalene breathing next to him.

"I'm sorry," she whispered. "I only hoped to help him see how happy and well suited you are for the directorship."

"It's no use. We have this same fight every time he sees me." Chandler rose. "Excuse me as well." *I'll show him if it's the last thing I do! Even if I must marry to keep the orphanage afloat, I will.*

❧

Magdalene watched Chandler leave the banquet hall, his shoulders drooping in defeat. She must do something to help—something to save the orphanage—something to help his father see Chandler's attributes.

"What can I do?" Magdalene glanced helplessly from her mother to her father.

"Pray for him," her mother said.

"I know, but I need to do something tangible, too. The orphanage has lost its funding. We won't survive another month without help."

"Then you need to draw public sympathy and attention. This city is full of wealthy people. Somehow, you must convince them to care about your cause."

Magdalene nodded, an idea forming.

"And we'll do whatever we can to help you," her mother reassured.

Magdalene smiled, loving them all the more.

As soon as she exited the banquet hall, Chandler told her

they needed to leave before a storm set in. They bid her family and his farewell, loaded up the buckboard, and headed home. The gray clouds hovering in the sky reflected Chandler's dismal mood.

After all the chores were done and the children tucked in, Magdalene sat down at the small desk in her room. Taking out pen and paper, she wrote a letter to the editor for the newspaper, hoping to draw sympathy and public attention as her father suggested.

She carefully folded the handwritten page and placed it in an envelope addressed to the newspaper. Then she grabbed her Bible and journal. Reading several psalms, she felt reassured God could, and would, take care of this orphanage. "Please give Chandler the same reassurance," she pleaded.

Chandler. . . Keeping him at a distance no longer seemed possible. How had she allowed him so much access to her heart and life in only two short days? Now, she not only knew him better, she knew his family—his tender mother who wanted God's best for him; his angry, single-focused father who resented his son's Christianity and life choices.

Run, Maggie. Run, my Maggie. Run. A smile settled on her lips as she thought back to his encouragement. Had he known he'd called her *my Maggie*? She'd nearly fainted dead away when he pulled her close against him, and they fit together like two puzzle pieces.

For the first time, she understood the pastor's sermon a couple of weeks ago about the husband-and-wife relationship. God had made Eve from Adam's rib. They fit together side by side. He wasn't made to lord over her or be tromped on by her feet. God created man and woman to walk side by side, he as her protector and provider.

Father, will there ever be a man to walk beside me? Her

heart ached with the answer she already knew to be true. Rising, she walked to her mirror and loosened the pins holding her hair in place. She stared at the woman standing before her and brushed her hair the usual one hundred strokes.

Fearfully and wonderfully made. The verse she'd memorized as a child whispered in her mind. She examined herself, biting her lip to keep the tears at bay. "I will praise thee," she whispered past the lump in her throat, "for I am fearfully and wonderfully made." No longer able to see herself clearly through the tears pooling in her eyes, Magdalene blew out her lamp and climbed into bed.

Heavenly Father, if that's true, why can't anyone see? Why am I invisible to any possible suitor? "Marvellous are thy works." She hoped saying the words aloud would make them truer. She fell asleep, repeating the verse over and over.

four

Chandler finished milking the cow. His frustration mounting, he kicked the milking stool aside. In the past three days since Thanksgiving, he'd found no one to donate anything for a ball. The public remained apathetic at best. Why, even at church yesterday, no one offered help of any kind.

Lord, I have no idea where to go from here. I'm all out of ideas, other than a marriage of convenience. He considered the trust fund his grandfather had set up for him. It held two stipulations: He must be twenty-five—that was the easy part—and married. He wondered how God felt about arranged marriages.

Carrying two pails of milk through the barn door and out into the foggy morning mist, he trekked up the hill to the house. Even Magdalene's support waned. She'd returned to her distant standoffish self.

Mrs. Lindsay opened the kitchen door and took the pails of fresh milk. "Fine mornin', ain't it?" she asked through a partially toothless smile. This woman would appall his father, but Chandler knew heaven sent her here.

He only nodded, unable to simulate enthusiasm. "Is Miss Fairchild up and about yet?"

"She's busy bathin' those young'uns. I'll have breakfast done right away, Mr. Alexandre."

"Thank you. I'll be in my office until then." First, he wandered up to the second floor—something he rarely did in the mornings. Magdalene tied bows in Susie's pigtails. "Could you come by my office before breakfast?"

41

Startled, she jumped and nodded. She'd reverted to the tight bun on her head, but he couldn't look at her without imagining brassy curls swinging freely in the breeze.

"As soon as I tie Sarah's pinafore, I'll be down."

"Thank you."

Moments later she entered his small office on the first floor. He looked up at her from his list of to-dos regarding the ball. Wearing another faded dress—this one barely yellow anymore—she sat across from him on the hard, wooden chair.

"What did you need?" Apprehension filled her words and the expression on her face.

"Have you started work on your ball list yet?" He didn't even try to mask his impatience. She'd said no to the same question on Friday, again on Saturday, and again on Sunday. Why would this Monday morning be any different?

She focused on her lap, where she fidgeted with the material of her dress. "No. I mean, I have done a couple of things, but nothing specifically for the ball."

"I mistakenly thought you cared about this place as much as I do." He rose from his chair. The legs scraping against the floor sounded as unpleasant as his words. He leaned over his desk toward her.

She cowered back. "I do. You know I do."

"How can I be sure, Magdalene? You're the one who always says a picture is worth a thousand words. The picture you're painting isn't a pretty one. Why do you hate the idea of a ball so much?" He wanted to understand and believe her.

"I hate rich people!"

He sat back down. "Why?"

"Do you remember when the Bank of California closed seven years ago?"

He nodded, remembering the incident well. It had affected

some of Mr. Baxter's and his father's holdings.

"My father held the position of president of the board of trustees. Mr. Ralston, the founder and main stockholder, found himself over nine million dollars in debt."

Chandler nodded, wondering if this had anything to do with today.

"Our money, like everyone else's, was gone. All my father had left was the mansion on Nob Hill. Instead of continuing in banking, he decided to sell the place and use the funds to return as much of the depositors' money as possible. He chose the right thing—the honorable thing."

Magdalene walked to the window. "But our neighbors suddenly treated us like white trash. They crossed the road when my sister Gabrielle and I walked down the sidewalk. Not one offered to help." Her voice cracked with the pain of the memory. "All our friends turned away. Rich people don't care about anyone except those who are just like they are." She faced Chandler. "They won't care about this old place or the children, either."

Realizing she was obviously deeply hurt by all that transpired, he tried to gently redirect her thinking. "I'm so sorry that happened to you and your family. I'm sorry people who claimed to care mistreated you. Maybe some of them have changed. How will we know unless we try?"

She returned to the straight-backed chair. "Do you know what I hate most in all the world?"

He shook his head, having no idea.

"Hypocrites and hypocrisy. You're asking me to rub elbows with those people simply to get money from them. You're asking me to pretend kindness I don't feel. I hate the way they treat people who don't measure up economically. Can't you see this is all wrong?"

Weary, he ran his hand over his cheeks and chin. "If there were another way, I would take it. I don't know what else to do." Frustration lodged itself in his throat, making speaking and breathing difficult.

The breakfast bell rang.

Magdalene rose. "I have a plan, Mr. Alexandre. The ball isn't coming together, anyway. I can tell by the defeated expression you wear, you've found no support."

She walked to the door and turned to face him once more. "We'll talk more tonight, but you'll be so surprised and pleased by then, I promise." Her eyes shone from excitement.

Oh, Magdalene, I do hope you're right. He forced a smile. "All right, Miss Fairchild, but we've already lost almost a week. If something wonderful doesn't happen today, we'll start on the ball tomorrow."

"Agreed." She opened the door to leave.

"Magdalene, wait."

She paused, hand still on the door.

"I'm sorry to ask you to do something you're not comfortable with, but we may not have a choice. This is for the children."

"I know. I'll see you at breakfast."

When Chandler joined her and the children at the table a few moments later, he worked to focus on the children and their antics, but his gaze continually roamed to Magdalene. Did she experience any of the emotions he felt when they were in close proximity to one another? If he had to take on a wife, would she consider the possibility, or was she called to singleness and determined to live this life alone?

❧

Magdalene waved; Chandler left in the little buggy for the city. He planned to go to the Palace Hotel, hoping they'd help with the ball, but she knew after her letter to the editor was printed today, their problems would soon be behind them. After all, she did just as her father suggested—sought public sympathy.

Magdalene went back inside the orphanage and called the children to the schoolroom to begin their studies for the day. Since the nearest schoolhouse was quite a distance and had only one teacher for over twenty students of various ages from six to fifteen, Mr. Baxter and Chandler decided schooling them at home would provide the best education, and both men placed high value on education. While Magdalene taught the older children, Mrs. Lindsay kept an eye on the smaller ones. "Bobby, will you start our day with prayer?"

"Our Father—"

A knock at the front door stopped him in midsentence. They rarely got visitors and never in the middle of the day.

"Please continue. I'm sure Mrs. Lindsay will take care of whoever is at the door."

Bobby rushed through the prayer, anxious just as all the children were to find out who might be calling.

"Amen," Magdalene said after his amen.

"Miss Fairchild, you best come quick." Mrs. Lindsay's panicked look caused Magdalene's midsection to tighten.

"Children, please write your spelling words each ten times. I'll return quickly. Until then, Mrs. Lindsay will see to it you stay seated and follow the rules." She glanced at Mrs. Lindsay with uncertainty.

"In the parlor, Miss."

Magdalene nodded and hurried toward the parlor. A couple sat on the horsehair sofa. He held a bowler in his hands, and she sat forward on the very edge of the couch due to her bustle.

"May I help you?"

"Are you Magdalene Fairchild?" the man asked, his Adam's

apple underscoring each word with a bob.

"Yes." An uncomfortable feeling crept over her. "What may I do for you?"

"We read your plea in the newspaper," the woman answered. "We've come to adopt a child."

The words stole the air from her lungs. "What?"

"This is the orphanage, isn't it? The San Francisco Home for Orphans and Foundlings?"

Magdalene nodded. These results weren't what she'd counted on—hoped for. Unable to stand on her weak legs, she sat down on the nearest chair. The woman shoved the paper at her, and Magdalene perused the beginning and ending of the article, skipping over the letter she'd written and knew by heart.

"We'd like your youngest child." The couple glanced at each other and smiled.

Frankie! They want to take Frankie. Think, Magdalene, think! What should I say? Dear Father, please help me.

"Miss, are you all right?"

Magdalene nodded, unable to speak.

"You're pale. Are you sick?"

She weakly shook her head, but she was sick—heartsick. Chandler had assured her before she ever took the job that children were rarely adopted in this part of the country. She'd counted on raising them until they were grown, never imagining facing this moment. Would these people love Frankie as much as she and Chandler did? Would they pray with him, tuck him in, and teach him about Jesus?

Another knock at the door brought her to her feet. "Excuse me."

She dreaded who might be out there. She opened the door, and a man with a camera flashed her picture.

"Miss Fairchild, I presume?"

She nodded, dazed by all that transpired. Never in her wildest imagination had she expected this.

"I'm Sam Starr. We plan to do a follow-up piece on the humanitarian story regarding the orphans. Can you bring them out for pictures? I'm all set up here on the porch."

She looked from the reporter standing behind his big camera, to the door of the schoolroom, to the parlor entrance. Leaning against the doorjamb, she silently cried out to God.

"You okay, Ma'am?"

Why did everyone keep asking her that? No, she wasn't okay!

"I'm sorry, Mr. Starr, but Mr. Alexandre, the home's director, is away on business this morning. Perhaps you should come back tomorrow, or better yet, not at all. I don't believe he'll want the children photographed."

"You can't send a heart-wrenching letter like yours and not expect a response."

The couple from the parlor came out into the foyer. "Miss Fairchild, when might we see the child we hope to adopt?"

Their words caught Mr. Starr's attention. "Excuse me." He pushed his way in past Magdalene. "Are you here in response to the letter in the paper?"

"Why, yes."

He pointed at his camera through the open door. "May I take your picture for tomorrow's edition?"

The couple glanced at each other with pleasure, nodded, and walked toward the camera; all the while, the reporter asked questions and made notes. As soon as all three were on the porch, Magdalene closed the door to a crack.

"I'm sorry, the director isn't available until tomorrow. You'll have to come back then." *Dear Father, what have I done?* Magdalene leaned against the closed door, over-whelmed. Already annoyed with her for not helping with the ball, this would ensure Chandler's disgust with her for the rest of her life.

Another knock echoed through the foyer, but she ignored it. Peeking through the front window, Magdalene saw two other couples talking to the reporter fellow. He flashed more pictures and wrote more notes in his little book.

After locking the door, Magdalene ran to the kitchen and did the same. Then she ran to the schoolroom and printed a large sign. NO ONE IS AVAILABLE TODAY. PLEASE RETURN TOMORROW. She longed to write, "No children are available for adoption, and please don't ever return."

Since all the adoption prospects had fallen through in the past, and since she and Chandler were both committed to coparenting these children until they reached adulthood, Magdalene had failed to emotionally prepare for this day. In the beginning, they'd faced the fact that the children would remain with them until grown.

She wanted the best for them, but how could anyone love these children as much as she and Chandler did? She'd read accounts of how adopted children were treated. The very thought sickened her.

When Magdalene opened the door to hang the sign, a different couple approached her. Nailing it up quickly, she slammed the door before they reached the porch steps. Mr. Starr appeared to be having a heyday, setting up his camera out front and interviewing all who came and went.

Magdalene closed all the drapes. Then she and Mrs. Lindsay shooed all the children upstairs, where they read and sang for the rest of the afternoon. An occasional knock still occurred, but she ignored them, only singing louder.

&

Chandler approached the Palace Hotel with both awe and resentment. Only a few years old, this—the biggest hotel in the country—cost five million dollars to build! What he wouldn't give for a small chunk of those funds to keep the orphanage going. He tended to agree with some of Magdalene's observations about the rich.

Passing through the large doors and into the lobby, he was struck by the luxury, present in even the slightest of details. Approaching the registration area, he overheard a clerk boasting, "A total of eight hundred rooms, Sir, on seven floors. They say society crosses itself in our corridors."

"May I help you, Sir?" a free clerk asked.

"I'd like to speak to your manager." Chandler hoped this trip would render success.

"May I give him your name?"

"Mr. Alexandre, Chandler Alexandre." He noted and disliked the clerk's impressed expression.

"Of the Nob Hill Alexandres?"

Chandler decided to own the family name if he gained admittance into the presence of someone who could help. "Yes, Archard is my father."

"Please make your way into the bar. Mr. Sullivan shall meet you there."

Chandler crossed the plush carpet in the direction the clerk had pointed until he reached a room foggy with cigar smoke. Bellied up against the polished rosewood bar sat important men from all walks of life. Some of them he recognized from his childhood. He knew his father closed many a deal here at the bar or in one of the private dining rooms.

Chandler perched on an empty stool near the end of the bar, as out of place as a horse hooked to a San Francisco cable car.

A newspaper lying on the bar a couple of stools down caught his attention. The headline just about knocked him off his seat. LOCAL ORPHANAGE CRIES FOR FUNDS, HELP. He prayed this wasn't Magdalene's answer to all their problems.

"Excuse me, Sir. May I borrow the paper when you're through?"

The man slid it down to Chandler.

"Thanks."

The older gentleman only nodded and took another swig of his beer.

Chandler read the article, feeling sicker with each word.

Local orphanage may be forced to close its doors before the dawn of 1883. What will happen to the dozen children who live within its walls? They aren't Jewish or Chinese, so they won't be accepted at either of the other two institutions. Below is a letter written to the editor by an employee of the orphanage, a Miss Magdalene Fairchild.

Dear Sir:

I ask you to find it in your heart to print this request for help. I'm not writing for myself, but for the twelve orphans I care for. There is little Frankie, who's never known another home or a mother other than me. Precious Susie's mother passed on after birthing her, and her father died at sea. Bobby and Sarah traveled from the East, losing both of their parents on the journey. All of the dozen have heartbreaking stories, and they deserve the security this home provides until they are old enough and can make lives of their own.

*I'm asking your readers to search their hearts
and ask themselves what they can do to help these
precious children avoid another tragedy in their
young lives. We will accept one time or monthly
contributions. We'll also accept non-cash donations such as food or clothing. Please, dear readers, search your hearts and find ways to help.*

> *Sincerely,*
> *Magdalene Fairchild*

*The paper, however, did further research, only to dis-
cover none other than Archard Alexandre's youngest
son, Chandler, runs the orphanage. If the Alexandre
money can't save this orphanage, then how can yours or
mine? Is this some kind of fraud? Maybe that's why Mr.
Alexandre is one of San Francisco's wealthiest. Perhaps
he hoards his money, unwilling to support the neediest
and poorest.*

*This reporter plans to get to the truth of this story. In
the meantime, maybe we need honest citizens to adopt
those youngsters and provide them with homes where
they won't be exploited for money.*

Stunned, Chandler laid the paper down. How could someone take Magdalene's letter and twist the truth like this?
*What will my father say when he reads the article? What was
Magdalene thinking? Didn't she realize the possible ramifi-
cations of her choice?*

Chandler didn't wait for Mr. Sullivan. He saw no use in
asking the Palace Hotel to sponsor a charity ball with all the
bad publicity from this article. They'd turn tail and run.

He headed home in a hurry, not sure what he'd do when he got there, but needing to get out of this city before he ran into someone who knew his father. *Dear Lord, I need help. How can I right all of these wrongs? I may not agree with my father on much, but I'd never want to hurt him or damage my family's reputation. I'm so angry with Magdalene. God, I need Your patience or I may say something I'll someday regret. And I need Your wisdom for my father's sake.*

Rounding the last bend before home, Chandler reined the horses to a halt. There were several buggies and wagons parked on the grounds. Some man had a camera set up in the front grass. Chandler clicked the horses and snapped the reins so they'd run the last leg home.

"What is going on here?" Chandler demanded as soon as he reached the chaos in the drive.

"Are you Chandler Alexandre?" The man asking the question stepped behind the camera and snapped his picture.

Chandler jumped from the buggy, aching to wring the guy's scrawny neck. It had been a day of disappointment, and he gave in to the anger building within. He grabbed a fistful of the front of the man's shirt. "Who are you, and what are you doing here?"

"I'm Sam Starr, Sir, and you are wrinkling my shirt." The guy was gutsy considering their size difference.

"Sam Starr, the reporter who wrote the lies in this morning's paper?"

"I calls 'em as I sees 'em."

Chandler's grip tightened. "You're a liar and sensationalist. Now get off my property, or I'll break that thing." He pointed at the camera.

Whoever the other people were, they quickly scattered to their buggies and left in a hurry.

five

Magdalene spotted Chandler from the bedroom window. "Stay with the children," she called over her shoulder to Mrs. Lindsay. She ran down the stairs, out the door, and straight toward him. He caught her in his arms, but quickly distanced himself from her, holding her at arms' length.

"I'm sorry! I'm so sorry!" When he loosened his hold, she fell against him, sobbing into his shirt. He stood ramrod straight, arms at his sides. The pounding of his heart echoed his anger. Magdalene backed away from him, wiping her tears on the sleeve of her gray cotton dress.

With trepidation, she raised her eyes to his face. Clenched teeth and a throbbing jaw muscle only confirmed what she already knew. Chandler Alexandre was livid and she was the cause.

"What were you thinking, Magdalene?" He spun away from her and raked his hand through his hair. "Do you have any idea what my father may do when he gets hold of that article?"

She nodded, a fresh spray of tears dampening her cheeks. "I only hoped to help."

Chandler turned back and faced her. "I gave you a whole list of things you could do to help. Did you bother with those?" His face reddened as he spit out the words.

She shook her head. Guilty and deserving his anger, Magdalene focused on the ground. "I'll start right away." She turned toward the house, but his next words stopped her.

"Don't bother."

"But—" She spun back around.

His gaze shot fire and his words seethed with anger. "What good will planning a charity ball do now? Who would buy tickets to support this place since Sam Starr's article has damaged our reputation? Why would anyone in his right mind support an institution accused of fraud?"

"Then I'll write to the churches in the area, as I'd originally planned." She raised her chin, determined to find a way to undo this mess she'd created.

Chandler shoved his hands into his pockets, shaking his head. A grim expression settled over his face. He let out a long breath, and with it some of the anger seemed to dissipate, but the hopelessness left behind wrenched Magdalene's heart.

"Our reputation is on the line." He spoke softly, in a monotone. "We're no longer a credible institution. No pastor or church will risk its money on us. Even our own church yesterday—before all the bad publicity—had little interest in helping us. It's over, Magdalene. We have no funds and nowhere to turn." His words pierced her heart with unbelievable pain.

Chandler turned and walked toward the orphanage. His shoulders drooped with the weight of his burden. The closing of the front door echoed the finality of their future.

Magdalene collapsed on the grass, tears cascading down her cheeks and sobs wracking her entire body. What was wrong with her? She rarely cried. Now, it seemed it was all she did. *Father, please help us. Forgive me for my impetuous action. I only wanted to help. . . .*

She'd never forget the anger marring Chandler's handsome face—the face she'd grown to love. He was hurting as much as she. Their world, their future collapsed around them. She'd planned to grow old here, pouring her life and care into needy children. He apparently had the same plans. Now, he surely must hate her.

Horse hooves on the road caught her attention. A shiny new black Calash rolled behind two bay beauties. The driver slowed the horses and reined them into the orphanage driveway. In the seat behind him sat Mr. and Mrs. Alexandre.

Magdalene yearned to turn and run, but instead stood and faced the approaching buggy. The Alexandres had never visited once in the three years since the orphanage opened, so she knew this was not a friendly, just-in-the-neighborhood kind of visit. No, they'd read the article and came to heap more guilt upon her head.

The driver nodded at Magdalene and pulled the horses to a stop. He then climbed down and offered Mr. Alexandre a hand as he exited. Chandler's father's beady eyes focused on her, rooting her to the very spot where she stood. Mr. Alexandre turned to help his wife down.

Magdalene forced herself to walk toward them, her resolve strengthening with each step. "Sir, Ma'am, I need to apologize for this mess I've made."

Mr. Alexandre appeared surprised by her approach, as if he'd expected her to turn tail and run. He only glared at her, but in Mrs. Alexandre's kind eyes, Magdalene spotted an ally.

"This is all my fault. Chandler had nothing to do with any of it. Why, he felt as surprised as you when he read the article earlier today."

His expression remained unmoved. "You're his employee. He is responsible for your actions."

"I only wanted to help, Sir. I'd never intentionally do anything to hurt Chandler, this orphanage, or your family. When Mr. Baxter died, we lost our funds. I thought if I could evoke public sympathy, support would pour in."

"You obviously thought wrong." His voice held a cold edge.

Magdalene bit her lip. If there were anything in her life she could undo, it would be this. Unfortunately, life offered no do-overs.

Mr. Alexandre walked past her, toward the front door. Grabbing his arm, she pleaded, "Please, Sir, I beg your forgiveness. Don't reprimand Chandler. This isn't his fault." The words spilled forth, filled with deep emotion and humility. He never turned back or even glanced at her. Instead, he knocked her hand off his arm like a pestering insect and strode toward the orphanage.

"I'll try to buffer the situation." Mrs. Alexandre stopped and patted Magdalene's arm. "I'm always the peacemaker between those two. I know you didn't intend to make this huge mess."

Magdalene nodded, appreciating the woman's kindness, but *huge mess* didn't begin to describe the havoc she'd sown.

"Are you coming?" Mr. Alexandre bellowed from the porch.

Mrs. Alexandre nodded her gray head, smiled an understanding smile, and squeezed Magdalene's hand. Magdalene watched her join her husband on the porch. *Father, please be with Chandler. Give him patience and wisdom, and enable him to forgive me for the pain I've caused him.*

❧

Chandler watched the scene unfold from his office window. He didn't want to feel compassion for Magdalene, but his heart responded to her bravery. Normally shy and unassuming, she faced them with courage and humility. Deep down, he knew this wasn't her fault, at least not directly.

His anger moved from Magdalene to his father when he observed the way he treated her. At least his mother had been there and treated Magdalene gently. His mother, forever the harmony seeker. He hoped and prayed she'd someday commit her life to Christ. She often seemed close.

Chandler moved away from the window and reached the front door just as his father pounded with fervor. He swung the door open, nearly catching a fist in the stomach as his father continued to pound.

"Father, Mother—how good to see you both." Chandler's voice dripped with sarcasm. "And what a pleasant surprise. So good of you to drop by after all these years to see where your son lives and works." All the bitterness from all the years of his father's disapproval rose within him.

"That's enough disrespect!" His father's face glowed red from his anger.

"Do come in."

His mother sent him a pleading glance, and Chandler led them to his office and closed the door. His father scrutinized the tiny room.

"Please have a seat." Chandler gestured to the two uncomfortable chairs facing his desk. Secretly, he took pleasure in thinking of his father sitting in one. Archard Alexandre had probably never sat on anything so atrocious in his entire life.

Chandler walked around the desk and settled in his own chair, not much different than theirs, except his rolled and Mrs. Lindsay had sewn a pillow for his seat.

His mother gingerly lowered herself on the edge of her seat, too much a lady to complain. She straightened the skirts on her floral-printed dress. Instead of sitting, his father stood behind the empty chair, his hands gripping the back.

"I know you've come because of the news article featured today, and I know Magdalene has already apologized profusely. What else can be said that hasn't already been said?" Chandler watched the pulse pound on the side of his father's forehead.

"You need to make this right!" His squinted eyes glared their disapproval.

"How?" Chandler rubbed his cheek and chin in frustration. "I've done nothing but think the entire day. I have no answers. What would please you, Father?"

"I want you to get the reporter fellow to retract his implications about me, then I want you to close this place down and come to work for me."

Chandler closed his eyes, taking a calming breath. It's what his father had always desired. A controlling man, he hadn't been able to manipulate Chandler, and the fact drove him crazy. Would he never give up?

"You know I can't. I have an obligation to these children." Chandler shook his head, knowing his father only used the situation for his own gain.

"What of your obligation to family? You've hurt your mother and me." He threw in his mother, knowing she was Chandler's Achilles heel. Chandler loved his mother deeply; she'd been his saving grace as he grew up.

"Father, there's been little in this life you and I have ever agreed on, but I would never intentionally damage our family name or your reputation. You have my word."

"Well, you did. Now find a way to make things right!" He turned on his heel and stormed out of the room.

Chandler's gaze met his mother's distraught one, and both jumped at the slamming of the front door.

"I'd better go. I don't wish to increase his wrath."

Chandler walked his mother to the Calash where his father already waited, tapping his foot on the floorboard. After a quick hug, his mother climbed aboard and they were off. Chandler watched until they disappeared around the first bend in the road. Then he strode to the barn, needing a quiet place to think.

In the stillness of the barn, the Holy Spirit brought conviction. Chandler still struggled with anger, even after eight years of knowing the Lord. In the strain since Warren's death, he'd spent too little time in the Word and too much time in worry. Warren would be disappointed that he'd fallen back into his old pattern. Even worse, God was disappointed.

"Lord, forgive me. I've failed You again. Lord, I know all the things taking place today do not surprise You. The question is, what am I to do? The orphanage's future is grim, and getting married may be the only hope of saving the old place. Is that why You provided me with the trust fund? Is it part of Your plan for my future?

He threw a pitchfork of hay into the cow's trough, then did the same for both horses. As his mind weighed the events of the day, immense disappointment filled him. He'd failed God so many times on this one short day.

He continued his prayer. *I need You to forgive the way I treated the reporter, Magdalene, and my father. I let anger get the best of me, and my actions failed to glorify You. Show me how to make things right.*

The word "forgive" kept dancing through his mind. Could he forgive his father for a lifetime of hurts? Could he forgive Magdalene for sending her letter to the paper without his consent? Could he forgive her for the repercussions he'd endured for her impulsive action? Both his relationship with his father and his future were bleaker, and she was responsible.

After Chandler finished with the animals, he moved up the hill to the house. He searched the first floor and couldn't find Magdalene. The children all read from their McGuffey readers in the schoolroom, but no Magdalene. Taking the stairs two at a time, he found her in the children's bedroom, rocking

Frankie. Her back to the doorway, she didn't see his approach.

She sang softly and ran her fingers through the child's dark hair. Her maternal side pulled Chandler's heartstrings as nothing else could have. An overwhelming tenderness surged through him. Watching her rock their littlest orphan, he knew she'd be a good mother to his future children, and she would willingly work beside him here in the orphanage. But he couldn't forget her sister's inviting look and lips. Would Magdalene ever welcome his kiss, his touch?

❧

Rising from the rocker, she laid a sleeping Frankie on his cot and glimpsed Chandler in the doorway. No longer foolish enough to run into those strong arms, she stood firmly planted next to Frankie. She pulled her lips together in a firm line. *Don't be fooled by the tender expression. Friends forgive friends.*

"Magdalene," Chandler whispered. "I need to see you in my office."

Nodding, she moved toward the doorway. "I'll check the schoolroom and be right there." Hurt and somewhat mad, her aloof attitude came easily.

A few moments later, Magdalene joined Chandler in his office. The sight of his head bowed over his Bible chipped away at the grievances she held against him. Upon hearing the door, he closed the leather-bound Book.

"I'm sorry for the way I treated you." He closed his eyes as if gathering his thoughts. "I'm struggling not to be angry with you, but even so, I shouldn't have behaved unkindly toward you."

Wanting to jump to her own defense, she refrained from saying anything and chewed her lower lip.

"I know in my heart—" he moved his hand to his chest

"—you meant no harm."

She focused on the floor. "I really didn't."

The dinner bell rang. She longed to turn and run for the table.

"Do you forgive my treatment of you earlier today?" He whispered his request in a raspy voice.

"Yes, and please forgive me for this huge mess."

"I do." He sent her a forgiving smile. "Dinner calls." He opened the door as the children ran past toward the dining room. "Walk," he warned them. Then he followed her to the table, took his seat, and acted completely normal.

six

The breakfast bell rang. He never normally lay in bed at this late hour. Unable to sleep, he'd not dozed off until the predawn light seeped through his window. Caught oversleeping, he jumped up and donned his jeans and a flannel shirt. Reality smacked him in the face when he remembered Magdalene's after-dinner warning last night that several couples were coming back today to adopt some of the children. How could they give any of them up? They'd never prepared emotionally for this possibility.

Sure, people came by on occasion, hoping to get a cheap laborer, but they never met the criteria needed to actually adopt a child. In cities, adoption was rare. Both he and Magdalene knew that. Somehow, they'd fooled themselves into thinking they'd nurture all of these children into adulthood.

Magdalene and the children were already seated at the table and waiting for him. He blessed the food, and they dug into eggs and sausage, but he could barely choke down anything.

The knocking started before they'd even finished breakfast. Chandler gave each couple paperwork to fill out, sending them into the parlor to accomplish the task. He pulled Magdalene aside and told her to keep the children in the schoolroom or upstairs. He didn't want them playing outside today with all these people coming and going.

She nodded, a somber expression filling her eyes. "Will they take them today?"

"No, I have to check into the legalities and do this properly.

I'll review their applications and maybe by next week some of them will be approved."

"I never planned to lose any of them." A lone tear escaped.

He fought an unexpected urge to wipe it away, remembering her soft vulnerability the night he'd found her crying up in the kitchen. "Me, neither. I thought we'd have them all 'til they were grown." He yearned to hold her in his arms, receiving and offering comfort, for his heart echoed the pain written across her face, the sadness woven through her words. "Well, I better get to those law books." *And away from you before I do something foolish.*

Chandler spent the rest of the morning in his office interviewing couples, reading over their forms, and studying adoption laws. None of the applicants seemed good enough to raise any of their children. The four named in the paper, Frankie, Susie, Bobby, and Sarah, were most requested.

Realizing their time together might be short, Chandler decided an afternoon at the beach was a much needed distraction for them all. At lunch, he made the announcement. The children were thrilled; Magdalene seemed both happy and saddened by the idea.

They dressed warmly. The sea air carried a chill this time of year. They trudged over the few hills between them and the ocean. He carried Frankie, and Magdalene held Susie's and Sarah's hands. The older children ran ahead, lagged behind, and scattered across the horizon. They knew the rules, though, and always stayed within sight.

❧

Magdalene looked out over the ocean, a powerful reminder to her that God was still in control. Thinking about this being their last outing together, all fourteen of them, nearly did her in. She must find something else to do, something to occupy her mind. She'd question Chandler about his family! Curiosity had nagged her since Thanksgiving. This might be her last opportunity to ask. By next week, they could all be heading in different directions, toward separate lives.

"Are you the only Christian in your family?" she asked as they settled into a comfortable position in the sand. Magdalene pulled her knees up to her chest, wrapping her full skirt carefully so she remained well covered. The older children raced away from the lapping waves. The three youngest worked on a sandcastle with Chandler.

"Don't get wet," Chandler warned. "You'll freeze. Yes, for now. I believe my mother is close."

"What prompted you to ask the Lord into your life? I know Mr. Baxter had a lot to do with your decision. . . ."

He sighed. Remembering seemed hard. "I was born early and almost died. I spent much of my childhood in bed, weak and unhealthy."

The news surprised her; he was the picture of good health.

"My mother and I were very close. She spent hours at my bedside, reading to me, teaching me, and being my companion. I'm the youngest of ten children and the sixth boy. My father didn't believe in *coddling* boys—as he called it—so he resented me and my relationship with my mother." He started another room for the castle, his much more sophisticated than the children's.

"Anyway, at eighteen, I met Warren Baxter, and he took a real interest in me—becoming the father I never had. He told me about Jesus and sowed seeds of truth in my heart. God watered those seeds and opened me up to Himself. Within months, I prayed the sinner's prayer, and Warren became my spiritual father. He discipled me until his death." Gloom shadowed Chandler's face.

"You miss him."

He glanced in her direction. "Very much. I wish he were here now to pray with me and guide me. I have no idea what to do, absolutely no idea."

"I'm sorry you're going through this because of me."

Compassion filled his face. "This may have come about anyway. I'm trying to remember God is sovereign. This is no surprise to Him, and He has just the answer we need."

Magdalene had to agree with him, though living out her faith proved much more difficult than just saying the words.

"Most things in life are for a season, Magdalene. Maybe the orphanage had only one short season and has served God's purpose. Maybe the best thing for these children is to have their very own parents. No matter how much we love them, we can't give them a family in the true sense of the word."

Magdalene felt uncertain whether or not she agreed with him. He and the kids sure felt like family to her, and she loved them just as much.

&

Upon returning to the orphanage, Chandler discovered another not-so-flattering article graced the front page of today's paper. A picture of him, clenched fist swinging in the air and an angry scowl plastered on his face, only supported the reporter's theory that depicted Chandler Alexandre as a violent man, unable to control his rage. The headline read, WE MUST SAVE THE CHILDREN! Why had he allowed his emotions free rein yesterday? Instead of crying out to God for self-control, he let his anger control him. Now he reaped the consequence of his choice. His reputation and that of the orphanage faced further scrutiny.

After dinner, he took a long walk alone, weighing the options before him. A marriage of convenience in order to obtain the money his maternal grandfather had left for him appeared to be his only alternative. No other possibility existed to support him or the orphanage. The likelihood of donations lessened with each newspaper article.

He sat on the cold, damp sand, listening to the waves crashing against the shoreline. The restless churning of the sea matched the emotions stirring within. *Lord, I need You so much. Direct my path. Show me the way. I'm weary and discouraged.* Chandler hadn't cried since childhood, but weeping before God tonight seemed a distinct possibility.

None of the applicants looked promising, either. Maybe he expected too much, but none of them had plans for religious teaching in the home. God was a Sunday activity. The rest of the week, they didn't give Him much thought. What chance did any of them have of raising godly offspring if He wasn't an important priority every single day and in every single choice?

In Chandler's mind's eye, he envisioned each of the children's faces. The lump in his throat increased in size, and unshed tears blurred the image of the ocean before him. He'd never allowed himself to consider the possibility of any of them ever being adopted. He'd planned to father them for the rest of their lives. Would moving on disrupt their stability, or would it be better for them to have a mother and father?

Chandler shivered, more because of his musings than the cold wind blowing on him. A million questions without answers plagued him. He rose and headed home. He needed someone to talk to—anyone. He missed Warren so much, he hurt. Who would even understand, except Warren? They'd shared a deep connection because of the Lord and their passion for the orphanage.

His mother! She always understood him. He jogged the rest of the way to the barn and threw a saddle on Stubby. He rarely rode and normally hitched the team to a buggy, but the thought of riding tonight beckoned to him. Luckily, Stubby was trained for both saddle and harness. The whistle of the wind blowing past him as he galloped along the road brought a sense of exhilaration and freedom, and for the duration of his ride, his troubles blew free.

He arrived at his parents' home just past seven-thirty. Though the lights still burned brightly through the window-panes, he knew they'd soon be turning in for the night. He hoped his father was out for the evening at some business affair or meeting and he could visit with his mother alone.

He rang the bell, and Baldwin answered almost immediately. "Mr. Alexandre, Sir, are you quite all right?"

"Quite, Baldwin. Is my mother in?" Chandler removed his leather riding gloves.

"Madam was just turning in. I shall see if she's willing to receive visitors."

Chandler nodded and stepped into the foyer to await the decision. Such formality. He'd never want a child of his feeling like an intruder. No, he always planned to be available, even if he earned a hefty salary as shipping mogul and lived in a house the size of a castle.

"Chandler, Dear." His mother looked concerned. "It's late. Is everything okay?" Her hair had been let down and braided for the night. She wore her sleeping attire.

Chandler nodded. "I need to talk. Do you have time to listen?"

"Always, Dear. Baldwin, please take Chandler's coat." She requested a spot of tea with cream and sugar. Having an English butler had rubbed off on the Alexandre household.

Afterward, she took hold of Chandler's hand and led him to a small sitting room where she received only her most intimate guests. "Now do tell what brings you out on this chilly December night."

Chandler stood and paced the length of the little room. "I don't know what to do about the children, the future of the orphanage, or Grandfather's will."

"Are you considering marriage?" his mother questioned softly, but he didn't miss the surprise in her tone.

Uncertain he wanted to broach that topic just yet, he changed the subject. "Where is Father?"

"He's in a meeting with your brothers to discuss future expansion."

Baldwin entered with their requested pot of tea. After placing the silver service on the cherry wood coffee table, he quietly left the room, closing the door behind him.

Chandler returned to his seat while his mother poured the precise amount of cream into each cup, then she filled the remainder with tea. "Sugar?"

At his nod she asked, "One lump or two?"

"Tonight I believe I need two."

She smiled, dropping two cubes into his tea and handing him the hand-painted rose china cup and saucer. "Tea fixes what ails. Now, shall we get down to business? I'm all ears." She raised her teacup to her lips, never removing her gaze from his.

Taking a deep breath, he plunged forward. "Do you think I should get married to save the orphanage?" He sipped the hot, sweet liquid.

"Who would you marry?"

"I have a quandary there. Perhaps Miss Fairchild."

"Which Miss Fairchild?" Her cup clanged against the saucer.

"That's my quandary, Mother. Do I marry the one most suitable to mother children—" He rose and strode to the fireplace, where he turned to face his mother.

"Magdalene?"

Nodding, he continued. "Or the one who looks at me with longing in her eyes—the one who'd be the most desirable wife." Surprisingly, his words brought memories of Magdalene to mind with her teary eyes and long hair falling loose around her, and his stomach churned in response.

"A difficult choice. Do you have feelings for either?"

He thought long and hard before answering. "I respect Magdalene. She's a hard worker, loving with the children. I admire her selfless attitude, but the way Isabel smiled and flirted, she made me feel like a man." Although in all honesty, lately Magdalene drew out his manly feelings of protection. Several times recently, he felt confusing, unnamed sensations in her presence.

"Sounds as though your emotions for Magdalene run deeper, but you like the way Isabel makes you feel."

Nodding, he said, "Exactly. I fear if I marry Magdalene, she'll never desire my touch. I wish for a real marriage. . . ." His face grew warm at the honest words. "Maybe I should forget the whole idea. All the children could be adopted out, and I could close the orphanage down."

"But that is not your wish." His mother knew him well.

He shook his head. "No, my wish is to keep going as things have always been, but little in life remains the same for any period of time."

"A lesson we all learn as we age."

"I can't bring myself to approve the current requesting families though they do qualify. They would be good families, just not the very best. I can't imagine life without those twelve precious faces to brighten my day." He rubbed the stubble on his jaw.

"Then why don't you adopt them yourself? You can afford a large brood of children with what your grandfather left you."

The idea hadn't occurred to him before, but maybe he and Magdalene could at least adopt Sarah and Bobby. Filling his lungs with air, he set his jaw in determination. "I'll do it, Mother—I'll marry Magdalene. She's the best choice for the children."

"I always loved your unselfish way of thinking."

Sighing, Chandler returned to his chair, sipping his now somewhat lukewarm tea. "The children, the orphanage, they are more important than my longings."

"I believe Magdalene will make the best wife. Isabel seemed young and spoiled."

He nodded, remembering her sulky display.

His mother continued, "I like Magdalene. I think she'd make a fine wife for you and a good mother to those twelve imps." Her eyes sparkled with the possibilities.

"She may well say no. She only tolerates me."

"Well, she does love the children, so offer her a marriage of convenience for their sake. Then work hard to win her heart. No woman can resist a handsome man and a good wooing."

Chandler rose and hugged his mother. "I hope you're right. How do you feel about inheriting another dozen grandchildren?"

"The more the merrier, but I'd like at least one who's yours and Magdalene's."

"Don't count on that, Mother. We have no feelings for one another."

"If there is one thing I've learned over almost forty-five years with your father, feelings have little to do with love. They come and go like the wind. Love is a choice, and you can decide to act on that choice with Magdalene."

"You speak as if she'd already said yes."

seven

His mother winked at him. "She shall."

Then after two brisk knocks on the door, his father entered. "A secret meeting?" His heavy brows rose with the question.

"No, Dear. Chandler just decided to pay us a visit." His mother always handled his father well. "One of his first questions was, 'Where's Father?'"

Archard accepted her explanation and visibly relaxed. He'd always been jealous and insecure because of the closeness Chandler and his mother shared.

Chandler rose and shook his father's hand. "Good to see you, Sir. I trust your meeting went well and that my brothers are keeping their noses to the grindstone, making lots of money for the family empire."

Archard bristled at his comment.

"I meant no ill will, Sir—only making conversation, not criticizing the family's ambition." Chandler paused for a moment, not sure how to begin. "Father, would you have a seat?"

He joined his wife on the small sofa. Chandler returned to his chair, perching on the very edge. "I plan to ask Miss Fairchild for her hand in marriage and then maybe adopt some of the orphans."

"The homely spinster?"

Chandler felt appalled by his father's description. "Miss Fairchild may be a little plain, but she's certainly not homely. How could you think of her as such?"

Father made a coughing, wheezing noise, but said nothing.

His mother raised her brows, sending him a knowing smile.

"Anyway, I'm hoping for your blessing on my decision."

"But she has no social standing."

His mother laid her hand on his father's arm to keep him from saying more.

"Father, you should know by now status is meaningless to me."

Archard exhaled a frustrated sigh.

"We shall plan a Christmas wedding." His mother—always the buffer between them—spoke up. Her enthusiasm confirmed she'd already given her blessing. "And what about a bridal tour? Where do you think—"

"Babette, the poor girl hasn't even said yes and you're sending them on a trip."

"Ah, but she will. Who could resist our handsome son?"

Chandler smiled, catching his mother's excitement. "Perhaps I should return home now and ask her." He rose and faced his father. "May I have your blessing, Sir?"

"You're marrying her for the money, aren't you?"

Wishing he could deny the truth, he said instead, "You know her family has no money."

"As you are well aware, I'm referring to that ridiculous inheritance your grandfather left for you." Agitation raised the volume of his father's voice. "I can arrange a more suitable marriage for you with someone more appropriate, more appealing."

Chandler hated the unspoken implication that Magdalene was beneath him. "I find Magdalene quite appropriate and appealing."

His father stood. "You do everything possible to cultivate my displeasure. If I approved, you'd want nothing to do with her!" He stormed toward the door, turning to face Chandler before he exited. "You have no blessing from me!" He shook his fist in the air to emphasize his words. He left, slamming the door.

Chandler turned toward his mother, pleading, without words, for advice.

She shook her head. "I wish peace for the two of you."

"I'm sorry. He makes me so angry."

"As you do him."

"With or without his blessing, I must do this. No lady from high society could love those orphans the way Magdalene does. They need her."

His mother nodded. "You need her, too."

"Yes, I need her to care for the children." Chandler hugged his mother and rushed for the door. Since he'd made up his mind, he planned to waste no more time. "No matter what Father says, she's the right person."

"Yes, the right one for you."

"Good night, Mother."

"Good night, my son."

Heading out into the night, he realized he aimed to do things right and must obtain Edward Fairchild's blessing before he proposed to Magdalene. Remembering Mr. Fairchild often fished at night, he hoped to catch him before he finished for the evening.

As Chandler rode Stubby along the roads leading to Rincon Hill, a nervous tension tightened his stomach. He spotted Mr. Fairchild and his son-in-law, Mr. Morgan, on the beach, cleaning their catch for the night. In the quiet of the night, their voices carried to him.

"I'll take them to market first thing in the morning so you can help Gabrielle with the children. Jacqueline mentioned Gabby's been ill of a morning." Mr. Fairchild grinned with pleasure.

"Number five's on the way, and we're just as excited as when she carried our first." Mr. Morgan grinned back.

Chandler dismounted and cleared his throat.

Mr. Fairchild jumped up. "Is Magdalene okay?"

"Yes, Sir, she's fine. I needed to speak to you a moment, if you don't mind."

"We're just about done here, so I'll take the rest up to the house. You can swing by and pick them up in the morning." Mr. Morgan rose to leave.

"I appreciate your obliging me," Chandler said.

Mr. Morgan nodded and bid them both a good night.

Chandler faced Mr. Fairchild, meeting his gaze square on. "Sir, I'm requesting your permission to marry Magdalene."

Stunned barely described the expression on Mr. Fairchild's face. He took a step backward, shaking his head in bafflement. "You've caught me by surprise. Does this have anything to do with the news headlines the past couple of days?"

"Yes, Sir."

Chandler explained everything to Mr. Fairchild, not certain the man appreciated what he heard.

"Sounds like nothing more than a marriage of convenience." He tied his boat down for the night.

"It would be, Sir." Guilt plagued him as he considered how the arrangement sounded. In a sense, he planned to use Magdalene to fulfill his goals.

"Have you mentioned this idea to her?" Mr. Fairchild asked, tying another square knot in the rope.

Chandler glanced down. "No, Sir."

"How does she feel toward you?" Mr. Fairchild stood, putting them back on eye level.

"I'm not certain." The guilt grew.

"I don't know what to think." Mr. Fairchild stared out over the sea. "Is this best for her?"

"I understand your hesitation, but we both love the children. I promise I'll provide for her and do right by her, if she'll have me. Will you give her the chance to make her own decision?"

He sighed. "She's always been levelheaded. I guess I can trust her to choose wisely."

Chandler's heart jolted. "Are you giving your blessing, Sir?"

Edward shook his hand. "Yes, Son, if she'll have you."

"Thank you! I won't disappoint you."

"Just don't disappoint her," Mr. Fairchild warned, "or you'll have me to answer to."

Chandler mounted his horse. He knew he should feel happy, but the huge responsibility of marriage was staring him square in the eye. He'd promised her father he'd do right by her. What if he failed?

"Godspeed, Chandler."

"Thank you. Sleep well, Sir."

With those words, he galloped off toward home and the woman he barely knew but hoped to marry. He'd cleared two hurdles tonight—just one more to go—Magdalene.

Lord, I pray I'm doing the right thing.

❧

Magdalene walked back and forth across the parlor floor, fear gripping her as she peered out the window again, hoping for some sign of Chandler, but only darkness greeted her. He'd disappeared right after dinner, and the clock now approached eleven; he'd been gone almost six hours. This was so unlike him. He'd never once in three years missed tucking the children into bed.

Trying to squelch the alarm, she returned to the Boston rocker and picked up her Bible. She attempted to concentrate on the words, but she'd lost her ability to make sense of them. Thinking she heard a noise, she ran to the window for another disappointment. A raccoon scurried across the porch.

She'd try praying again, though she hadn't succeeded on her last dozen attempts. What if something awful had happened to him? "God, please let him be fine. Please be with him."

She'd barely gotten through the children's bedtime routine without her emotions betraying her. Now they were all asleep and she had no more strength left for bravery. Her body quivered with anxiety. If she had someone to stay with the children, she'd go search for him, but Mrs. Lindsay went home hours ago.

At the first light of dawn, she'd begin hunting for a sign of him. She'd get her father and Nathaniel to help. Unable to remove from her mind the horror of a man who'd drowned last summer, her terror spiraled. Right before his wife's eyes, the undertow won the battle and he disappeared. Days later, his body had washed up on shore. *God, please don't let Chandler be dead.*

At the sound of hoof beats, she raced to the window. Chandler rode Stubby across the yard toward the barn. When had he gotten the horse? He'd left on foot. Relief washed over her. After wiping her damp palms on her apron, she ran her hands over her hair, hoping she didn't appear as disheveled as she felt. She paced the floor, repeatedly thanking God until she heard Chandler's boots clomping across the porch. Stopping, she held her breath.

The door opened and Chandler strode in without a care in the world. Undecided whether to throw herself in his arms and hug his neck or to wring his neck, she did neither.

"Magdalene! I didn't expect you to be up this late—"

"You thought I could sleep not knowing if you were dead or alive?" How dared he act as if sauntering in halfway through the night was normal and acceptable!

"I'm sorry. I never thought you'd worry."

"I've been half out of my mind!"

A silly grin nearly split his face in half and infuriated her even more. He moved across the foyer toward her, reaching for her hands, but she turned her back on him, crossing her arms over her chest. "This is not funny, Chandler Alexandre."

He seemed undaunted by her fury. Grabbing her arm, he pulled her around to face him. "Does this mean that you maybe care about me a little?" He placed his hands on her shoulders, forcing her to stay put.

"Of course I care! You can't work with a man for three years and not care about his well-being."

"Then marry me."

Surely her hearing must be acting up. "What?"

He knelt in front of her, sliding his hand down her arm and holding her hand. "Marry me, Magdalene."

Weak in the knees, she thought she might faint dead away. Apparently sensing her unsteadiness, he stood and led her to the rocker, gently seating her before kneeling again.

"My mother's father left me money in his will. The only stipulations were my age and that I have to be married to collect." He walked away from her, rubbing the back of his neck. Facing her from across the room, he continued. "I don't know how else to save the orphanage. Maybe we can even adopt some of the children ourselves." He walked toward her. "I can provide you a good life. We'll have more money than we have now and can fix this house up any way you please."

She sat in stunned silence, scarcely able to absorb all he said.

"I'll work hard to be the husband God would have me be. I'll provide for you and protect you all the days of my life." He paused to take a breath. "I can make you happy, Magdalene, if you'll let me try."

Her mouth hung slightly open, but not a peep came out.

Unable to form thoughts or words, she just stared at him. His confident expression grew uncertain.

"I talked to my parents and your father. He gave his blessing on our union, if you'll have me."

"You talked to my father? And he gave his blessing?" Her father knew as well as she did that this would be her only chance at marriage, so he gave his blessing to a man who didn't love her.

"At first he was about as shocked as you are, but when we talked things over, he said he trusted you to make the right decision—he mentioned your being levelheaded."

"And your father would allow you to marry me?" Doubt emphasized her question.

Chandler glanced away for a brief moment, and she knew he'd not received his father's blessing. "No. He'd prefer I close the orphanage and go to work for him."

"I'm sure I'm not good enough for his son." *Or pretty enough.*

Chandler took her hands in his. "That doesn't matter, Magdalene. It's my decision, and besides, you're the one those twelve orphans would choose if they could handpick their own mother."

It really came down to the orphans. She swallowed her disappointment. "A marriage of convenience?"

"Of course. I'm under no delusion that you love me."

"Or you, me."

"But you said you cared about me, and I certainly care about you. Maybe in time we'll grow to love one another."

"And if we don't?"

"We'll have a good life—not much different than the one we have now, except you'd be Magdalene Alexandre."

She pulled her hands from his and rose. "I need time to think. This is happening much too fast." Rushing toward the stairs like a scared rabbit, she looked back before she ascended the first step and was taken aback by the desolate expression on his face. "Good night, Chandler." Not waiting for his response, she nearly ran full speed to her room. *If only he'd mentioned love as one of the reasons we should marry, and if only he didn't appear completely miserable over his proposal.*

Preparing for bed, Magdalene avoided the mirror, not wanting to be reminded of why Chandler would never love her. She didn't even bother with her hundred strokes but climbed into bed, hairpins and all. Numb, she stared out her window at the black, starless sky. Though she didn't cry, on the inside wept a homely woman whose dream might partially come true, but no joy came with the knowledge.

Not knowing when she fell asleep or if she even did, Magdalene rolled out of bed as soon as she heard Mrs. Lindsay enter the kitchen to start the breakfast preparations, even before the sun rose. "I must talk to Gabrielle," she told the pale woman in the mirror, before rushing to ready herself. She'd ride into town with Mrs. Lindsay. The woman normally did their weekly shopping on Wednesdays and wouldn't mind dropping Magdalene off at her sister's.

Tiptoeing past the children, Magdalene took the creaking stairs as slowly and quietly as possible. Needing some time to herself for thinking, she bundled in her wool coat, deciding an early morning walk would clear her mind. She left through the kitchen door, asking Mrs. Lindsay for a ride to town and to keep an eye on the children.

Once outdoors, the crisp air invigorated her senses. She glanced around the old place, the home Chandler offered to her in exchange for taking his name and vowing to love, honor, and obey. . . .

A girl could do worse: a handsome husband, maybe some

adopted children, a home of their own. She closed her eyes. The only problem was, she yearned for his heart, for his love. Could she settle for second best?

⋅◐⋅

Chandler spotted Magdalene through the trees. She must have needed fresh air as well. He ducked behind an oak, certain he'd be an unwelcome intrusion. Watching her, he relived the pain of her almost-rejection last night. He'd known she didn't love him, barely liked him for that matter, but her anger and worry over his disappearance gave him a sliver of hope.

She admitted to caring about his well-being, but he cared about Mrs. Lindsay's well-being, for heaven's sake. He wouldn't marry the woman, though. Magdalene's feelings for him were no different than one might have for a neighbor or an acquaintance—certainly not the stuff marriage was made of. Had he made a huge mistake even asking?

He'd offered this place as if it were some sort of prize. Looking at the homestead he loved, he wondered if she saw worn-out buildings or a place filled with possibility, a place to build dreams.

Remembering the dejected expression that crossed her features when she guessed his father's reaction to their possible upcoming nuptials brought a stronger ache to his heart. Why did she care what Archard Alexandre thought? Why did he?

He hadn't expected her to swoon and fall into his arms, nor had he expected her to react as if he'd offered to pull a tooth from her mouth. In truth, her response left him filled with despair. The idea—when it came to him last night—seemed the perfect answer for all concerned, but in the light of morning, he wished he could retract the words and erase them from her memory.

He'd lost track of Magdalene. She'd walked out of his line

of vision, but a quiet whimpering verified her closeness. There she stood, her raised arm resting against a large tree trunk, and her forehead lying on her forearm. Her quiet sobs reminded him he was the reason she wept.

"Magdalene?" He approached her with quiet respect.

She turned. The sight of her tear-streaked face ripped a hole in his gut. He wrapped her in his arms, knowing a wiser man would have left her undisturbed. She rested her head on his shoulder.

"I will retract my proposal, if doing so shall stop your tears." Without thinking, he stroked her hair in a tender gesture. "I never meant to upset you. I only desired to keep the orphanage from being closed." His fingers curled into the silky strands of her bun, aching to remove the pins when he remembered the way it looked down and free. He closed his eyes, and his lips reverently touched her temple.

"I know you meant no harm, only good."

She pulled back to look at him, and soft vulnerable lips drew his gaze, which he quickly averted.

"May I have the day off?"

Her request knocked him off balance. Did she plan to go to town and find a new job? Would she desert him when he needed her so much? He backed a step away, leaving her with a confused expression.

"Take as much time as you need." His quiet words reflected his disappointment. Turning on his heel, he headed toward the barn to start his chores. She called his name, but he didn't respond, didn't want her to see the betrayal he felt.

eight

Mrs. Lindsay dropped Magdalene off at the bottom of the hill, and she wound her way up the trail to Gabrielle's cottage. She hadn't spoken to Chandler again before she left for the city. Her request for the day away made him annoyed. Would she never understand him?

He hadn't come in for breakfast, saying he had to finish all his outdoor chores before she and Mrs. Lindsay left for the day. Then he'd stay inside with the children. He hadn't come in until moments before they left, and seeing him brought fresh pain to her heart. How could they marry when she knew how deeply her feelings ran and how shallow his were?

Climbing the steps to Gabby's door, Magdalene thought of how often she'd dreamed of marrying a man like Nathaniel and living in a cozy cottage like this one. She knocked once and opened the door. "Gab, it's me."

"Mag!" Gabrielle rushed to her and embraced her in a tight hug. "I've missed you! I have news. Do you have news?" Gabrielle's sky blue eyes twinkled.

"You first," Magdalene encouraged, wondering how she might know there was news. Of course it wasn't every day she just dropped in for a visit.

Taking hold of Magdalene's hand, Gabrielle placed it on her tummy. "Number five!" Her face glowed.

"You're with child?"

Gabrielle nodded, and both sisters screamed and jumped up and down.

"What in the world?" Nathaniel entered the room carrying

the twins, one on each hip. "Magdalene, she told you our news?"

"Yes, and I'm thrilled." She lifted her hands and the twins lunged toward her. Laughing, she hugged both little girls close, carrying them to the rocker near the fireplace. "Auntie Maggie loves her girls," she said, kissing first Faith and then Grace's chubby cheeks. As soon as she sat down, both girls scooted to the floor, toddling back to Nathaniel's waiting arms. A picture of her and Chandler sharing a bundle of their own came to her mind, and with the thought, a piercing sorrow because he didn't truly love her.

"Honey, I'll take the children for a walk so you and Magdalene can visit in peace." A knowing look passed between the couple.

"Let's go in the kitchen. I'll brew some tea, and you can share your news."

Magdalene followed Gabrielle into the bright yellow, very homey kitchen. Taking a seat at the table, she asked, "What makes you so certain I have news?"

"Nothing." Gabrielle took two teacups from the cupboard, giving Magdalene a knowing grin.

"Gabby!"

"Oh, all right. I never could keep anything from you." She joined Magdalene at the table. "Your nosey sister and brother-in-law are dying to know why Chandler came by late last evening to speak to Father."

Magdalene sighed. "He asked for my hand."

"And my, but aren't you overjoyed by the prospect. Were you two courting?"

Shaking her head, Magdalene updated her sister on all that had transpired since Thanksgiving.

"Wow, in less than a week? No wonder you look exhausted."

"I am. I'm not sleeping well, if at all."

The teakettle steamed, and Gabrielle finished the preparations. "You picked your way through all the facts of the story, but never mentioned feelings. Tell me what you're thinking and how you feel about Chandler Alexandre." Gabrielle studied her for a moment when she returned to the table. "You love him, don't you?"

"Very much, and he loves the children."

Gabrielle squeezed Magdalene's hand. "Love can grow over time. Think of Mother and Father—their arranged marriage blossomed and flourished. Just like you, Mother actually loved him before the ceremony."

Magdalene strode to the window. "I yearn for what you have." She turned to face her sister. "A man who loves me so much, he can't bear the thought of living without me. If only I were beautiful like you, then I know he'd love me." Gabrielle's pale blond hair and clear blue eyes had turned men's heads for longer than Magdalene could remember.

Gabrielle hugged her close. After a few moments, they both sat back down. "Magdalene, beauty isn't everything and certainly doesn't guarantee happiness or success. All my life, I never knew if anybody liked me for myself, especially the boys who called on me. Often, courting a beautiful woman feeds a man's pride.

"And let's face the facts, you're a much nicer person than I was back then. I'd gotten into the habit of using my looks to get what I wanted, and my appearance almost cost me Nathaniel."

"What do you mean?" Magdalene had a hard time believing beauty could be detrimental to a relationship.

"He'd vowed to avoid beautiful women because they were much too selfish and self-centered. He saw me as an empty-headed, vain woman, and if God hadn't gotten hold of my heart and changed me, Nathaniel Morgan would never have married me.

"And speaking of God, He created you, Magdalene. He knit you together exactly how He wanted you. He chose every detail to make you uniquely you, and He loves you so much, He's counted every hair on your head. So what if every man doesn't fall at your feet? The God of the universe is enthralled with you. You're His bride, and one day your Prince will come riding a white horse to take you and each one of us home with Him to heaven, just as His Word promises in Revelation."

Gabrielle's wisdom touched a broken place in Magdalene's heart and brought hope. She was a treasure to God. A warmth flooded her soul.

"I learned those truths the hard way." A humble, grateful smile lit Gabrielle's face. "Just like you, I thought what I saw in the mirror determined my worth, but God looks at the heart. My value comes from Him, not this face of mine. Now with that settled," Gabrielle said as she hugged her sister, "are you going to marry Chandler?"

"I've prayed, and I'm just not sure it's the right thing to do."

"You've prayed for years for a husband and family. Now a godly man—whom you happen to love—is inviting you to be his wife. You must consider the possibility that God is answering your prayer. Nathaniel says God's answers rarely come in the form of our expectations."

She hadn't taken into account the likelihood of Chandler's proposal being heaven sent.

"Let's consider the whole picture," Gabrielle continued. "I assume you and Chandler have been praying for the orphanage and children?"

Magdalene nodded.

"If Chandler marries you, the problem of losing the orphanage is solved, and your long-time prayer is answered. The circumstances all point in one direction.

"Nathaniel taught me to discern God's will in three ways. You look to the Bible and make certain everything lines up with His Word. Marrying Chandler doesn't go against Scripture as long as you honor the marriage covenant and follow the guidelines set for wives."

"Of course. If I marry him, I'll be the best wife I can be." *Then maybe he'll love me.*

"The second is prayer. You've both prayed, and getting married certainly provides answers to several prayers. Another thing to weigh is circumstances, and all the circumstances point toward marriage as the answer."

"What choice do I have, anyway? If not for my letter to the paper, Chandler may have found other means to support the orphanage. I ruined all possibility of that. It's the only way I can rectify my mistake."

"And you love him. I really believe this is God's provision for both of you."

Gabrielle—always so sure of everything in life. Magdalene, on the other hand, rarely felt sure of anything. She rose and sauntered the length of the kitchen. Taking a deep breath, she declared, "I'm going to say yes." Then in a choked whisper, "Pray he'll grow to love me." But inside she had no faith in that happening. How could he ever love someone like her?

"I will." Gabrielle squeezed her hand "You're a wonderful person, Magdalene. When Chandler gets to know you better, he won't be able to keep himself from loving you."

Oh, how Magdalene wished she could believe Gabrielle's words. "I think I'll walk over to tell Mother and Father. Will you join me?"

"I need to stay here and start dinner. Nathaniel and the children should be back soon, and they'll be ready to eat."

After bidding her sister good-bye, Magdalene headed down the well-used path to her parents' cottage. Her mother, father, and Isabel were just starting to eat their noon meal and asked her to join them. After taking helpings of roast, potatoes, turnips, and cornbread, Magdalene mentally prepared to make her announcement.

"Father, I understand Chandler paid you a visit last evening."

Her father nodded, studying her face as if searching for answers.

Magdalene sent him a tiny smile. Not wanting the whole world to know Chandler didn't love her and this marriage was only for money, she tried to sound excited. "Well then, I have an announcement to make." She plastered a large smile on her face. "Chandler Alexandre and I are to be married."

"Wonderful, Dear!" Her mother's sincere smile held no surprise, but of course Father would have told her about Chandler's visit last night.

Isabel glared at her. "You know I'm in love with him! How could you do this to me?"

"Well, he loves me!" Magdalene cringed as the lie poured from her mouth. "And I love him!" At least that part was true.

"You didn't love him last week. You're only doing this because I set my hat for him."

"I did love him last week. I just don't discuss my private business with everyone."

"So, you let me make a fool of myself?"

"Girls, enough arguing!" their father reprimanded. "When's the big day?"

"We haven't decided for sure. Probably Friday."

Her mother choked on her food. "The day after tomorrow? Magdalene, why the rush? Don't you want to give me time to plan a small family wedding?"

"We've been waiting a long time." Another lie, and the second easier to tell than the first. "Why, I think I've loved him since the first day I moved to the orphanage. We're both more than ready." And they were, but not because of love. *Father, forgive my lies. I can't bear being pitied.*

"What about a gown?" Her mother's disappointment showed.

"I can wear the blue one Isabel sewed for me."

"I won't marry in a plain dress like that," Isabel assured them.

Magdalene ignored her. "I imagine we'll marry in the afternoon. I'll let you know, but count on sometime Friday. I'm supposed to meet Mrs. Lindsay at the bottom of the hill at one, so I'd better run. Thank you for the meal, and I'll send word." She hugged her family good-bye, thankful there wasn't more time for talk of weddings, brides, and gowns, finding the subject made it difficult to remain upbeat.

The jolting ride home on the buckboard jarred her nerves. Feeling nothing like an excited bride, she dreaded telling Chandler of her decision. Was it worse to be an old spinster or to marry a man who'd never love her? And what if he'd changed his mind? The thought mortified her, since she'd told her entire family of the upcoming event.

❧

Chandler and the children played croquet on the front lawn. They all ran to the buckboard to greet Magdalene and Mrs. Lindsay when they rolled in. As Chandler lifted Magdalene down, touching her caused unexplainable havoc with his senses. "Why don't you children help Mrs. Lindsay carry in the goods? Miss Maggie and I need to talk."

After the children, the supplies, and Mrs. Lindsay disappeared into the orphanage, he led Magdalene to the swing on his porch, where they settled in beside each other. Taking her hand, he tenderly stroked the velvet smoothness of her skin. "I need to apologize for my behavior this morning."

She nodded, but said nothing.

Swallowing hard, he said, "I want to reassure you—if you agree to marry me, I'd be a good husband, try to be tender with your feelings, and treat you well." He stood and paced to the other end of the porch, raking his hand through his hair. "Last night, you seemed almost insulted by my proposal." He walked back toward her.

She stood and faced him. "Shocked, not insulted."

"In the light of day, I guess getting married seems like a crazy idea." He took her hands in his.

"Yes—yes, it does." She raised her chin a fraction. "But in the light of day, I accept your proposal." She nervously licked her lips.

A giddiness started in the pit of his stomach and rose within him. This meant he could keep the orphanage running. "You're saying yes?"

At her nod, he grabbed her by the waist and swung her around, his relief huge. "You won't be sorry, Maggie. I promise you that." He stood her back on the porch.

After planting a quick kiss on her mouth, he grabbed her hand and dragged her along as he sprinted to the orphanage, where the kids and Mrs. Lindsay were putting away supplies. He rushed through the kitchen door, Magdalene behind him. "We're getting married," he shouted. "Miss Maggie and I are getting married!"

The children cheered, and Mrs. Lindsay hugged Magdalene. Both women cried while he and the children danced around the room.

"Uncle Chandler," Bobby whispered. "Why is Miss Maggie crying? Shouldn't she be happy?"

Chandler chuckled. "Women cry when they're happy, cry

when they're sad, and sometimes they cry in between."

Mrs. Lindsay hugged him. "You have us all figured out, don't you? You keep her tears to a minimum, understood?"

"Yes, Ma'am. I'll do my best." He hoped he could.

The girls all huddled around Maggie, chattering about dresses and weddings.

"Children, I'm going to borrow Miss Maggie for another few minutes. We have much to talk about. Why don't you finish the game of croquet without me, and Mrs. Lindsay can prepare our supper without you underfoot."

All twelve of them made their way out the door, Bobby taking responsibility for Frankie, as he often did. Chandler and Magdalene walked side by side, going nowhere in particular. He stopped and faced her. "Tomorrow? Can we do this tomorrow?"

"Friday. A girl needs at least a day to plan. My mother is already sad she can't help with a wedding and heartbroken there'll be no gown."

❧

Magdalene thought she might drown in those midnight blue eyes of his. He pushed the loose tendrils of hair away from her face, and she shivered at his touch. "I wish we had time to do this right and make all your dreams come true, the wedding, the dress, everything, but we need to get the money as soon as possible."

The money, always the money. For brief moments, she felt happy, but then he'd remind her why they were doing this. For the money. . .

"This is a great sacrifice for us, Magdalene, but God will bless our efforts. Remember, He said what we do for the least of these, we do for Him."

She nodded. *He considers marrying me a great sacrifice.* His words cut deep into her heart. Of course it would be.

After all, he could have done much better had he had the time to court another. What if he ended up hating her? This was all her fault. If only she'd never written that dumb letter!

He stared intently. "What are you thinking?"

She looked away, off toward the ocean on the horizon. She gave voice to her fear. "Could this loveless union be our secret?"

"Not loveless, Maggie," he whispered. His words nearly stopped the beating of her heart, and she liked the way she felt when he called her *Maggie*.

"Not?" Her gaze returned to his tender expression and hope grew.

He shook his head. "We both love the children with all our hearts."

Hope crashed. "We do, at that." She forced a brief smile. "I'd like to speak to our pastor and make certain we aren't breaking any of God's laws. I don't want a union built on sin." *Just fraud and deception.*

"The church will be our first stop tomorrow. Then we'll file the paperwork for the will and invite both families to the ceremony. I thought it best if we did this at the church rather than having a house wedding. Or perhaps here."

"I'd never considered this place. Let's decide tomorrow, so both our mothers might have a say."

"I like the fact you are selfless and caring."

"As are you." *If only you could love me. . .*

He bent to kiss her, and her heart responded with pounding delight. As their lips parted, the expression on his face left her woozy. If this wasn't love, it might be the next best thing. Maybe this wouldn't be so bad, after all.

nine

Magdalene's wedding day arrived and resembled nothing she dreamed of as a little girl. No joy filled her heart, no anticipation—only a deep sense of obligation and a profound sadness that she'd soon be joined to a man who didn't love her.

She stared at her pale, unsmiling face in the mirror. A weeping heart pounded within her chest, and tears pooled in her eyes, threatening to spill over onto her cheeks. She didn't want to cry. Wearing a blue cotton dress as a bride was bad enough, but having a red nose and blotchy skin would only increase her humiliation. No, she would not give in to tears or self-pity.

A knock on the door startled her. Chandler had promised no one would bother her until the wedding. "Who's there?"

"Us," her mother's and Gabrielle's voices answered in unison.

Gabrielle opened the door and carried in a wedding gown. "Chandler asked us to bring this up."

Magdalene swallowed, fighting more tears. "For me?"

They both smiled and nodded.

Running her fingertips over the soft, ivory satin, she admired the simple, yet elegant, gown. "Where? How?"

"Chandler borrowed it from one of his sisters." Gabrielle glowed with her excitement.

Probably from Nadine—the large-boned, sturdy one.

"Your father explained the situation to me, Dear, and I want you to realize Chandler will be a good husband. Not many men would understand the importance of a gown to a bride." Her mother took the dress from Gabrielle and laid it across Magdalene's feather bed.

"I'm sure he was just embarrassed by the thought of marrying a girl in ordinary, blue cotton."

"Magdalene, what a terrible thing to say." Her mother looked aghast. "He's trying. The least you can do is appreciate his efforts."

"You're right, Mother. I'm sorry. It's a beautiful dress and a kind gesture."

"Let's get you into it and be certain it fits. Then Mother and I will fix your hair. I even brought fresh flowers and silk ribbons to weave through it."

The gown fit like someone made it just for her. She could hardly believe she was the woman in the mirror.

"Oh, Magdalene, you are a beautiful bride." Her mother's eyes got misty.

"Truly, you are," Gabrielle agreed. "The ivory is a much better color with your complexion than stark white would have been. Now come sit over here, and we'll start on your hair." She turned the chair just so.

Magdalene did as instructed.

"Chandler has his mother and sisters downstairs getting the children ready. You should see them!" He'd obviously won her mother's heart.

"Apparently he borrowed clothes for them, too," Gabrielle said. "And Mother's right—they are all adorable."

"I know these aren't the circumstances a girl plans to get married under, but he's attempting to make today special for you." Her mother desperately tried to convince her of his gallant efforts.

"You're correct, Mother. He's a good man, but I don't wish to love him anymore than I already do. Don't you understand how painful living with him will be, knowing he feels nothing for me except duty because of some vows he felt forced to make due to my careless actions?"

Gabrielle and her mother glanced at each other, but neither said any more. Gabrielle worked to get Magdalene's thick, curly locks into an upsweep with small ringlets around her face, ears, and the back of her neck. She kept it much looser than Magdalene normally did, and the effect was softer.

A knock reverberated on the door. "Magdalene, Dear, it's Chandler's mother. May I come in for a moment?"

Gabrielle quickly opened the door. "Please do."

Magdalene heard Mrs. Alexandre's sharp intake of breath. "You look wonderful, Dear. Chandler shall be most pleased when he catches his first glimpse of his lovely bride."

Magdalene smiled, aching inside for her future mother-in-law's prediction to come true. "Thank you," she whispered.

Her future mother-in-law took hold of Magdalene's hand and placed a long, thin box in her palm. "I wanted to welcome you to our family. This belonged to Chandler's great-grandmother. She gave it to me the day Archard and I sailed away from France."

Magdalene's hand shook slightly as she lifted the lid. A beautiful cameo on a burgundy velvet choker lay inside the box.

"Won't it look lovely with the ivory gown?" Mrs. Alexandre asked Gabrielle and Jacqueline.

Both agreed, and Gabrielle lifted the heirloom from the box, securing it around Magdalene's neck. Magdalene walked to her mirror, fingering the fine piece of jewelry. *God, I pray Chandler will be pleased with me and grow to love me in time. . . .* Determined not to cry on this day, she'd not dwell on her petition. Instead she admired the gown and the cameo, hoping Chandler might someday admire the girl wearing them.

"Chandler made a good choice, asking you for his wife—a decision I'm convinced he won't regret. I wanted to reassure you, I'm your ally, Dear. I encouraged my son to pick you, certain you're the best woman for the job. Our family welcomes you, and please learn to disregard Archard—his gruff exterior is far worse than he actually is."

Magdalene forced a gracious smile to her lips, but felt sick inside. Bits of Mrs. Alexandre's conversation stuck in her brain. Repeatedly she heard the words, *Chandler made a good choice, asking you. . .a decision I'm convinced he won't regret. . .I encouraged my son to pick you. . .best woman for the job.* Had Chandler hoped to marry another?

"May I borrow your mother and sister a moment? I'd like them to come and see the way we've decorated."

Magdalene nodded, relieved they'd all be gone so she could stop pretending. When they left, she dropped into the chair, feeling worse about this wedding with each moment.

Inspecting herself in the mirror, she said, "Thank You, Lord, that I'm fearfully and wonderfully made. I know because all Your works are wonderful." The words sounded like lies. Why, she was no more thankful for her hair, her nose, her mouth, or even her face than she was for the sharks in the ocean. Gabrielle insisted *as a man thinks, so is he.* She promised if Magdalene said the words aloud to God each day, in no time at all she'd truly appreciate just the way He made her, flaws and all.

"Miss Maggie! Miss Maggie!" Sarah, Susie, Hannah, and Rachel rushed through the door. "Uncle Chandler says we can walk you down the stairs and bring you to him!"

Excitement danced in all four sets of eyes, ranging from blue to brown and a couple of shades in between. They admired her dress, carefully touching the satiny skirt, and she could hardly believe how beautiful each of them looked, wearing fancy party dresses and ribbons in their hair.

"Miss Maggie, you look so pretty."

"Prettier than ever!"

"Can I wear your dress when I'm a bride?"

"Will you kiss Uncle Chandler?"

They all talked at once, and Magdalene found their enthusiasm contagious, brightening her mood considerably. She pulled them all to her and hugged them tightly. *For them. This is for them.* Taking a deep breath of determination, she stood straight and lifted her chin. "I'm ready. Lead the way."

Sarah ran to the balcony and shouted, "We're coming."

Magdalene heard their guests laugh at the child's antics. Magdalene was glad the children came upstairs. They made the smile on her face genuine. A few moments later, her father joined them. He placed Magdalene's arm through his and walked her down the staircase. Sarah, Susie, Hannah, and Rachel walked ahead of them, dropping flower petals as they went.

"The flowers are from Mrs. Alexandre's garden," Susie informed her in a loud whisper. "And we gots flowers everywhere."

≈

Chandler waited for Magdalene at the bottom of the stairs, his heart pounding in anticipation. He realized somehow in the past couple of days, Miss Magdalene Fairchild had captured his attention. When and how had that occurred? Maybe his interest had always lain dormant just under the surface, and getting to know her better had brought his feelings to the forefront.

He caught his first glimpse of her on this, their wedding

day. His breath left his body in a whoosh. He wondered if she felt beautiful, because she certainly appeared so to him. His gaze never left her as her father and the girls escorted her down the steps. She'd been transformed, and the result left him weak in the knees.

Finally, her eyes met his, and she gave him a shy look and tiny smile. Did she feel all the craziness inside her that he did within him—almost as if dozens of firecrackers exploded throughout his body? Taking her hand, he led her toward the minister. Could everyone in the room hear the *rat-a-tat-tat* of his heart?

He glanced sideways at her, liking the way her hair hung in tiny ringlets around her face and the way she looked in Nadine's gown. They stopped in front of the fireplace, and Pastor Barnes prayed. Then he began the ceremony.

"We are gathered here to join this man and this woman in the union of holy matrimony, a union ordained and sanctified by God. Chandler, God commands you to love your new wife as Christ loves His bride, the church. Never in all of Scripture is Magdalene told to love you, but you are told several times to love her."

Chandler nodded, praying he could. *Maybe you already do,* a little voice whispered within.

"Do you know why God never exhorts Magdalene to love you? Because a wife reflects her husband as the moon reflects the sun. If you love her, she'll love you back. It's that plain and simple."

Then the pastor focused on Magdalene. "Do you know what God asks of you? He asks you to be Chandler's helpmate, to work beside him, complement him in his endeavors. Can you do so here in the orphanage or wherever God leads you in life?"

Chandler heard her gulp as if attempting to swallow her

fear, her nod barely perceivable. He squeezed her hand a little tighter, hoping to reassure her that somehow they'd do this together.

"Do you, Chandler, take Magdalene to be your lawfully wedded wife to love, honor, and cherish from this day forward in sickness and in health, in riches or poverty for as long as you both shall live?"

Now it was his turn to swallow hard. He was vowing to love her and he didn't, did he? "I do."

"And do you Magdalene. . ."

Shutting out the repetitious words, he prayed, *Dear Lord, help me. Fill my heart with love for this woman.*

"I do." Magdalene spoke hesitantly.

Glancing in her direction, he saw all the uncertainty and guilt he battled with written across her face.

"Remember, the biblical mandate of love is action, not feelings. No matter how you feel at any given moment, you're called to love as Jesus did. His love was always followed with action. Christ did rather than said. Chandler, you'll prove your love for Magdalene by the way you treat her and the priority she has in your life." The minister paused, smiling encouragement at them. "I now pronounce you man and wife, and you may now kiss your bride." He sent them an encouraging smile.

They turned slowly toward one another, Chandler's gaze steadfast on her lips. He lowered his head, aching to taste the sweetness of her mouth. His arms tightened around her, drawing her closer. She rose on tiptoe to meet him halfway. Their second kiss made the first pale in comparison. Long, deep, and slow, he put all he had into this one, hoping to calm her fears. When he raised his head, they were both slightly breathless, and a rosy flush covered her cheeks.

Magdalene knew her face glowed red; she felt the heat burning her cheeks. His kiss—enough to make a girl faint dead away.

As they walked toward the foyer, Magdalene saw the room for the first time—before, she'd focused solely on Chandler. The staircase had been decorated in pine boughs and red flowers as had the fireplace. With Christmas barely three weeks away, they'd used it as the decorating theme.

Chandler stopped in the foyer by the front door, and their guests began to file past, wishing them well. By the time the last guests greeted them, Magdalene's face hurt from smiling. Other than Chandler's father, who was noticeably absent, and Isabel, everyone seemed genuinely happy for them.

All of their guests had gathered on the front lawn, where tables and chairs had been assembled. They waited patiently for the bride and groom to go through the cake line first.

"Mrs. Lindsay insisted on baking a cake—said no wedding is complete without one," Chandler informed Magdalene as one of his nieces handed them each a piece of cake.

They visited with their guests another hour or so. "My mother has a surprise for us, which includes a buggy and driver," Chandler whispered in her ear, and she felt goose bumps dance across her spine at his intimate gesture. "Are you ready to leave?"

"I shall be in a moment; however, I need to run up to my room and gather my bag."

Magdalene rushed up the steps, stopping just outside her door, startled by the voices coming from her private domain.

"I knew it! I knew he didn't love her," Isabel stated with certainty. "A man doesn't look at a woman the way he did me just last Thursday and marry another eight days later."

"Quiet down, Isabel! I only heard my grandmother whispering the truth to my mother after Mother questioned her. Uncle Chandler's inheritance is common knowledge in the family, but they'd kill me if they heard me telling you he doesn't love your sister."

"Of course he doesn't. He loves me."

"Now, I didn't say that! I simply said Mother said he struggled to decide between the two of you. He ultimately chose Magdalene because of her ability with the children."

Magdalene leaned against the wall, feeling like a team of horses had just run over her.

"Josephine, think about what you're saying. If he married her for the children, then his only reason for considering me must have been love. I hate my sister for stealing him!"

Unsure if her legs would carry her, Magdalene rushed back down the stairs, Chandler stopping her at the doorway. "My, aren't you the eager bride," he teased. "Where's your bag?"

He glanced at the stairway Isabel and Josephine descended and gave Magdalene a questioning frown. "I'll get it."

She nodded and strode outside to avoid facing her younger sister. She found most of the children on the front lawn with all Chandler's nieces and nephews. Hugging each one goodbye, Chandler joined her and did the same.

On their way to the buggy, many of their family members threw rice. Chandler helped Magdalene in and climbed up next to her. The driver slapped the reins against the horses' hindquarters and they jolted forward.

Magdalene tried to ignore the hurtful words she'd overheard but couldn't erase them. A loveless marriage was bad enough, but a loveless marriage to a man who loved his bride's own sister—that was one hundred times more difficult to bear.

Dear God, I beg You to give me the strength to endure this horrible mess I've gotten myself into.

"Your father wasn't in attendance today," Magdalene commented after a few moments of silence.

"No. He's often conspicuously missing from certain family events. This isn't the first one he's boycotted, nor will it be the last."

She didn't want his absence to matter to her, but it did. He must know the truth—that his son loved Isabel.

Chandler took her hand in his large, work-roughened one. "Please don't let his actions upset our day. We've all come to accept this is the way my father is. Don't take it personally."

She stared at their interlocked hands. Dare she believe him? His father's absence felt very personal to her. Tears pricked the inside of her eyelids, but she would not give in to them.

"Do you know where we are going?" She needed a safer, less painful topic.

"No. My mother was sad for you that there'd be no wedding tour, so she arranged this little surprise."

Horror struck her. She pulled her hand from his. Surely they didn't expect her to. . . No, Chandler had said nothing would change except her name. He knew theirs was an in-name-only arrangement.

Neither spoke again, but Magdalene spent the rest of the ride into town fretting. If he'd married Isabel, she surely would. . . Her cheeks heated up thinking about it, but Magdalene couldn't—wouldn't.

The driver rolled to a stop at the Palace Hotel. Magdalene had only been there once, the first year it opened, but its size and wealth intimidated her then as they did now. All seven floors were built around a grand court. Chandler lifted her from the buggy. Their eyes met, his expression tender. She attempted to swallow her fear and uncertainty. He was a good man—of that she was certain.

He seated her on a crushed gold velvet chair and went to check them in. Everything here reeked of wealth, from the plush carpet beneath her feet to the ornate carved ceiling above her head. Women draped in jewels and silk paraded the halls. Suddenly the truth dawned on her: She was now one of them. She'd just married into the Alexandre family—a family far richer than the Fairchilds had ever been.

How ironic life turned out. Gabrielle yearned to marry a rich man, and she had no such desire. Now here she was an Alexandre and Gabrielle, a fisherman's wife. Some things made no sense.

Chandler returned and escorted her to one of the five elevators, which lifted them to the seventh-floor bridal suite. The entire room was quite striking, decorated in hues of lavenders and purples. Magdalene found herself drawn by its romantic beauty. Dark mahogany furniture in the Chippendale style graced the room. Damask patterned wallpaper covered all the walls, and a fireplace sat at one end of the room. A sofa for two and a couple of chairs were placed intimately around the hearth.

One massive canopy bed dominated the room—just one. Magdalene glanced at Chandler, wondering if he'd noticed, but he was busy tipping the bellman. Taking a deep breath, she hoped to calm her quaking insides.

"Well, what do you think?" Chandler asked her when the door closed and they stood alone in the center of the room.

ten

In her eyes, he saw the answer to his question. She didn't feel joy, but fear, uncertainty, and even sadness.

She turned away from him, facing the fireplace. "The room is quite lovely." Her words were stiff and formal.

He massaged her rigid shoulders, hoping she'd relax, but she only grew more taut. When he turned her around to face him, the stark terror in her eyes startled him. "What is wrong, Magdalene?" He lifted her downcast face so their gazes would meet.

"Nothing." She looked away.

It was a bald-faced lie, and he knew it. "You look exquisite." He reached up, removing a flower from her hair and handing it to her. He'd never seen a more beautiful sight than her today.

"You don't have to say that." Before she turned away again, he caught a glimpse of gut-wrenching sorrow in her eyes. She moved a few steps away, and he didn't stop her.

"I remember you telling Sarah a woman doesn't need to be told by a man that she's beautiful because it's an attitude she feels in her heart. Well, today you must have felt lovely, because you surely are."

She didn't answer or respond. He repositioned himself, standing inches from her, noting the pained expression on her face and the fact that her eyes were squeezed tightly shut. Something had happened when Magdalene went to retrieve her bag—something having to do with Isabel and

Josephine. Chandler had no idea what, but something had happened.

This was his wife, and he wanted her to feel safe, protected, cared for. He reached for her, pulling her into his embrace. Holding her tightly against him, he felt the pounding of her heart, heard the shallowness of her breathing. He cradled her head against his chest—his own heart hammering at her nearness.

His hand slid to her hair, removing first one hairpin and then another. Soon her hair cascaded over his hand and arm like water over a waterfall. He felt her tremble in his arms. Why did she fear him?

Taking her face in his hands, he kissed her eyes, the tip of her nose, and then his lips found their way to the fullness of hers. She wrapped her arms around his neck and clung to him, kissing him with as much ardor as he'd packed in his kiss.

After breathless minutes and several kisses, he lifted her and carried her to the bed. Soon she'd be his wife in every way. . . .

Magdalene bolted up and ran across the room. Her alarmed expression accused him of treachery. "You said the only thing between us that would change would be my name! A marriage of convenience is what you promised." Her shrill voice shook with emotions he couldn't name or understand—not after the way she'd just kissed him.

"You're my wife! Surely you didn't plan to live upstairs with the children?"

At her nod, he ran a frustrated hand across his jawline. Amazed, he'd just assumed. . . "I'm a healthy, red-blooded male. I've waited twenty-six years for this day."

She clutched her hand at her throat but said nothing.

"You weren't planning to move into my cottage?"

"I don't know. I hadn't thought that far ahead. Would I be expected to—?" Dark red raced up her neck and face, her skin matching the colored light outside the bordello down by the waterfront.

"No! Not if you don't want to." He couldn't believe this was happening. "Why did you kiss me like that if you didn't plan to follow through?"

She stared at the floor. "I just got caught up in the moment. I'm sorry."

He took a step toward her, and she backed against the door.

Now angry, he shouted, "I won't force myself on you, if that's your concern."

He sat down on the bed, needing to gain control of his rampant emotions. After several deep breaths, he rose and faced her where she still cowered against the door. "Magdalene, you're the one who doesn't want anyone to know this isn't a real marriage."

"I will not give myself to a man who doesn't love me—a man I. . .don't love either."

"Fine!" He stormed toward the door, and her eyes grew big as saucers and filled with terror, watching him move closer. She shrank against the door when he reached for her. "Don't worry, Magdalene. I won't make the mistake of touching you again." He gripped her upper arms and lifted her from in front of the door. Leaving her with mouth gaping, he exited and slammed the door behind him.

This woman married him for one reason and one reason only—guilt. The knowledge didn't sit well with his masculine pride or his heart.

❧

Magdalene crumpled on the bed. The tears she fought to

keep at bay all day finally won the battle. Had she made a horrible mistake? He may not love her, but even in her innocence, she realized his desire for her. Even worse, she recognized hers for him.

When he'd kissed her, she'd wanted nothing more than to go on kissing him forever. She'd just experienced the most incredible moment of her entire existence, for in his arms, she truly felt alive for the very first time. Maybe she should have taken what rightfully belonged to her as his wife and not worried if he wished she were Isabel. A seed of doubt took root in Magdalene's heart.

She fell asleep after hours of tears, prayers, and "if onlys." Chandler had not returned and though her stomach growled for dinner, she wouldn't risk the humiliation of running into someone who might question why she was alone on her wedding night.

Sometime in the middle of the night, she awoke and forced herself to step outside her room to see if she could spot Chandler somewhere below in the grand court. All was still and quiet. Only a few guests mingled among the palm trees. Raising her eyes to the translucent glass dome above, she silently cried out to God, *Please let him be okay.*

Returning to the room, she changed into her flannel gown. After she climbed under the covers, more tears flowed as she grieved over the lonely disaster her day had become. How she wished for her room upstairs in the orphanage, with children to hug and someone to hold her.

❧

When Chandler awoke the next morning stiff, cold, and achy, Magdalene filled his every thought. He stretched, rubbing his sore neck. After walking for hours, he'd tried to sleep on a park bench, forget his hurt and disappointment, and forget her kisses.

Remembering those kisses curled his toes, and holding her in his arms felt like heaven on earth. Any doubts whether the distracting thoughts about her were brought on by love fled when their lips had met. He was crazy about this girl from the top of her head to the bottoms of her feet. And she feared and despised him.

She didn't share his feelings at all. The kisses embarrassed her, made her uncomfortable, almost ashamed. *Now what, Lord? I finally find the girl I yearn to spend forever with, and she doesn't seem to share my longings. I'd be much obliged if You'd change her heart.*

A marriage of convenience, she'd asked. "Only for you, Magdalene. Only for you," he whispered, wishing he possessed the courage to tell her the truth about how deep his feelings really ran, but the words would only make things between them more awkward. He'd tell her someday. . . .

He yearned for her to be his wife in every sense of the word but knew that might never happen. Could they live together in the little caretaker's cottage beside the orphanage with him loving her from afar? Would he be content with that?

The sun crested in the eastern sky. He walked, stiffly at first, back toward the hotel, stopping to buy some fruit from a street vendor. Neither he nor Magdalene had eaten—unless she did so after he left—and his stomach protested loudly.

Quietly entering the room where Magdalene still slept, he thought she looked lost and alone in the big bed. He moved toward her, wishing for the freedom to hold her and kiss the frown line away. She'd apparently been restless, for the bed was quite mussed and her hair spread wildly across the pillows. He'd grown to love that mop of untamed locks. She rolled over and moaned, a pain-filled sound that constricted Chandler's heart.

Her eyes opened and for one dazed moment, she gazed at him with such longing, he nearly ran to her. Then a wall went up, hiding her emotions, and in a cool, controlled voice, she asked, "Will you take me back to the orphanage?"

He nodded, needing to say a million things but saying nothing at all. She gathered the sheet around herself and headed for the water closet. Coming out some minutes later, she was dressed in another faded dress, hair tight against her head in a severe bun, and deep pain residing in her eyes.

"I'm ready."

He could barely stand the icy tone of her words. "Magdalene, we have to talk."

"There is nothing to say."

He paced the length of the room. "What happens now?"

"We go home and continue this charade." Bitterness oozed from her statement.

"Is that what you want?"

"I just want you to leave me alone!"

Enough said. She'd not have to ask him twice. He carried their bags downstairs, where their buggy and driver still waited.

❧

Magdalene sat as far away from him as possible on the short buggy seat. She wondered if the driver sensed the tension between them and if Chandler wished he'd chosen Isabel instead.

On the ride home, she realized for the sake of the children things needed to appear as normal as possible. They'd have to be kind and respectful to one another, but that was all.

When they swayed to a stop at the orphanage, everyone—including Mrs. Lindsay—ran outside to greet them.

"Miss Maggie, we have so many surprises for you and Uncle

Chandler!" Sarah could barely contain her secret, first grabbing Magdalene's, then Chandler's hand. "Come see."

Surrounded by loud, excited children, Magdalene and Chandler were led to the cottage. Mrs. Lindsay and the children had cleaned, rearranged, and moved all of Magdalene's things to Chandler's home. Even a sprig of mistletoe hung above the door.

After they'd given them the tour, all the girls squealed as they passed under it, "Kiss her!"

Chandler looked to Magdalene for direction, and she knew he remembered his promise never to touch her again. With a slight nod, she gave permission for him to follow the children's orders. He planted a quick, chaste kiss on her mouth.

"Not like that," Susie protested. "The way you kissed at the wedding."

Her heart jolted. She longed to be kissed one more time the way he'd kissed her last night, the way he'd kissed her at their wedding. Chandler stood frozen, so she took the initiative. Leaning toward him, she pulled his head down to meet her halfway. His lips were reserved, apprehensive, but when they touched her mouth, she still felt that familiar ache for him to love her.

When she loosened her hold on his head, he quickly stepped away. She couldn't read his expression because he avoided eye contact, lifting Susie into his arms. "Is that good enough for you?" She nodded, giggling, and he placed a loud, smacking kiss on her cheek. The other three girls crowded around him, and he had to give them all equal attention and kisses.

Magdalene took the opportunity to wander back into the cottage alone. Looking around, drinking in the details of her new home, she ran her hand across the brand new wedding ring quilt Mrs. Lindsay had stitched. It covered the bed she and Chandler were expected to share. Tears collected in her eyes, and a lump lodged in her throat. Now she had no choice except to live here with him. She'd sleep on the horsehair sofa and make the best of a bad situation that grew worse each day.

"Magdalene?"

She hadn't heard him approach and quickly wiped her cheeks before turning toward where he stood in the bedroom doorway. "Where are the children?"

"I asked them to give us some time alone together, so you could get acclimated to your new home."

She nodded, glancing around the bedroom, avoiding his probing look to the best of her ability. "Thank you."

"I'm sorry. I had no idea they'd move you in here." He appeared as uncomfortable as she felt.

"I know. They were only trying to help."

"I'll sleep on the sofa. You can have this room. I won't bother you. You have my word." His sad smile pulled at her heart.

"It's your bed, Chandler. I wouldn't feel right—"

"Maybe we'll just take turns as we encourage the children to do." Another ghost of a smile turned up his handsome mouth.

"All right."

"Tonight, the bed's yours. I work late most nights, anyway."

"What about the children? Who'll hear them if they cry out in the night?"

"Mrs. Lindsay will move into your old room. I'll give her your salary on top of what she already earns. She can use the extra money, so it will help us all." He paused and, for a moment, she thought she saw extra moisture in his eyes.

"Magdalene, I'm sorry." He focused his gaze downward, so she couldn't actually see his face. "If I'd known what a mess this would turn out to be, I'd never have suggested this marriage. I thought it was the right answer, but apparently I was sadly mistaken, and now I've ruined both our lives."

"Chandler—"

He held up his hand to stop the flow of her words. "No need to say more. Just so you know, I'm deeply, deeply sorry." His voice wavered slightly. Clearing his throat, he said, "I have to meet with Sam Starr today and try to redeem my father's good name, so I probably won't see you until supper tonight. If I'm not back, eat without me." With those words, he left the cottage.

"I'm sorry, too. So sorry," she whispered, but it was too late, for he'd already gone.

❧

Chandler left on Stubby, knowing he'd purposefully miss dinner. He'd caused Magdalene enough pain and hadn't missed the fact she'd been crying when he found her in his bedroom. *Lord, please forgive me for making such a mess of things.*

He'd arranged a meeting with the reporter the day before their wedding, so Chandler found himself back at the Palace Hotel bar, waiting for the man who'd added to his already problem-filled life.

"Sam Starr at your service, Mr. Alexandre. What can I do for you?" The small man offered his hand and Chandler shook it, prayerfully determined to control his anger during this meeting.

"Mr. Starr, I'd like to buy your lunch and talk about a possible retraction regarding your article that insulted my father."

"I'd prefer to buy my own lunch. Then there is no mistaking

lunch as a bribe, and I feel no obligation to change anything unless you present facts that sway my opinion."

"Fair enough." Chandler held his tongue. He'd reserved a private dining room, and the mâitre d' led them there.

"Why should I retract anything?" Mr. Starr asked once they were seated.

"Because what you said about my father simply isn't true. He does support several worthy causes, just not my orphanage, and in all honesty, I've never asked him for a dime."

A waiter knocked, entered, and took each man's order.

Once he left, Chandler continued, "I hope this is off the record, but my father and I don't see eye to eye on my career choice. He'd prefer I work for him and since I don't, he doesn't want much to do with the orphanage. I prefer that myself, because if he were a donor, he'd want a say in how things are run."

Sam Starr nodded. The waiter returned with coffee for the reporter and hot tea for Chandler. Both men remained silent while they added cream and sugar to their steaming cups.

"I understand you married Miss Fairchild yesterday."

Taken aback, Chandler wondered how this man got his information. "Yes, I did, but that has nothing to do with salvaging my father's name and reputation."

"Was it another attempt to save the orphanage?"

"I married Mrs. Alexandre because I love her." Chandler looked him square in the eye, daring him to think otherwise. This was the first time he'd spoken the words aloud, and it felt good to say them. A smile softened his next words. "She's a good woman, and you were unfair to misinterpret her letter the way you did."

"I'm a reporter. My job is to uncover the facts and give them to the public."

"But things are rarely as they seem."

"Don't I know that! So you have a rift with your father, and my article made it worse. Now you're hoping I'll print a nice piece on his generosity and benevolence, so that you can redeem yourself slightly in his eyes."

"Actually, I'm hoping you'll just retract your implications about him, stating his youngest son desired independence and never asked for help."

Their lunches arrived. Chandler bowed his head, gave thanks for their food, then cut into his steak, waiting for Mr. Starr's reply.

"What's in it for me? How about an article on marrying for reasons other than love?"

Chandler fought his urge to wallop the man. *Lord, help me to stay calm.* "I wouldn't know much about the topic."

"Or marrying to collect on your grandfather's will?"

Chandler balled his hand into a fist but kept it in his lap. "Mr. Starr, either you're willing to retract your statements or you aren't."

"I am. Only I'd like a new piece with some sensationalism to increase newspaper sales."

"Then why don't you write about reporters who ruin people's lives by only reporting half truths?" Chandler knew he was close to hitting this man square in the jaw. Suddenly, he felt the Holy Spirit rein him in. The word "humility" kept floating through his mind.

Taking a deep breath, Chandler apologized. "I'm sorry. I lost my temper there for a moment. Mr. Starr, I love my wife, and she's been through so much because of your pen, I'm asking you, please don't make our lives more difficult. Please don't hurt her any more than she's already been hurt.

"Take your potshots at me if you must." Chandler rose and

circled around the table. "Print what a horrible son I've been, rejecting my father and his offer of a good job in order to work as an underpaid orphanage director. Sensationalize my life all you want, but don't hurt Magdalene."

"You really do love her." Sam Starr sounded amazed by his discovery. "Let's finish dinner." When Chandler returned to his seat, Mr. Starr continued. "I'll apologize for the paper and myself regarding our printed error about your father. I'll place the responsibility on your shoulders, and I'll even refrain from printing the scandalous story told to me by your wife's sister."

Chandler laid his fork down, stunned by the news. "Isabel?"

"A reporter never reveals his source. Now do you want to hear what I want in return?"

Nodding, Chandler felt dread settle in his stomach.

"Frankie."

"I beg your pardon?"

"My sister and her husband are one of the couples who filed paperwork to adopt from your orphanage. They want Frankie."

"I can't do that unless they qualify."

"That's fair enough, but why haven't you processed the paperwork on the dozen or so couples who filed to adopt?"

"Mr. Starr, do you have children?"

"I'm not married."

"I haven't processed the paperwork because I don't know how I can let them go. Magdalene and I both love those kids with our whole hearts."

"You're asking me to do the right thing, the honorable thing, and yet is that how you're running your orphanage?"

The answer stuck in Chandler's throat. He'd dishonored God because of his own selfish motives. "I guess not."

"You process the paperwork fairly, and I'll write no more

articles on you, your wife, or your orphanage, other than to publicly apologize to your father."

Chandler nodded his agreement. "What's your sister's name?"

"Leah. Leah and Roger Farnsworth."

"I'll see to it they get a fair shot at Frankie."

"Just so you know, I'm an evenhanded man, and they were the first couple to arrive at the orphanage the morning you started accepting applications. That should give them first rights—if they meet the qualifications."

"Good enough." Chandler barely choked down the rest of his food. How could he ever tell Magdalene his heartbreaking news?

When they'd finished dinner, both men passed on dessert. Sam Starr shook Chandler's hand. "Best of luck, Chandler. I'll print the retraction tomorrow, and just for the record, I never meant to harm you or Mrs. Alexandre, only to get at the truth."

Oddly enough, Chandler believed him.

He spent hours walking and leading Stubby along the beach. He prayed God would get him through the next few days and give both him and Magdalene the strength to say good-bye to some of the children.

eleven

Magdalene lay awake, listening for Chandler to come home. He didn't return for dinner or the children's bedtime rituals. Mrs. Lindsay expressed her concern that Chandler was staying away from his new bride for so long. Magdalene knew they hadn't fooled the woman for a minute. Truly, they hadn't fooled anyone, except perhaps themselves for the briefest length of time. Now they both seemed to be paying a high price for their foolishness.

Finally close to midnight, Magdalene heard the front door open and the sound of Chandler's boots as he crossed the wooden floor. She rolled over, her back to the door, feigning sleep, just in case he peeked in on her.

The bedroom door opened, and she forced herself to breathe in an even cadence, keeping her eyes closed against their will. He must have removed his boots, for his feet barely made a sound as he walked around the bed. His fingers ran lightly over the length of her hair, and he whispered her name. Soft lips lightly touched her cheek, and he pulled the covers more tightly around her. Then she heard the door close behind him.

A wisp of hope blossomed in her heart. He'd included her in his nightly ritual with the children—the one he did faithfully just before he turned in for the night—only he'd included a kiss with hers. His secret gesture touched her in ways nothing else could have.

&

Magdalene and Chandler followed their normal Sunday morning routine as if nothing abnormal or unusual had happened since last Sunday. In one short week they'd faced horrible public accusations, a wedding, a disastrous wedding night, and numerous other problems.

When Chandler and Magdalene arrived at church, many in the congregation made a special point to congratulate them on their marriage. Chandler—ever the gallant knight—kept his arm about her shoulders and gazed lovingly into her eyes from time to time, making it easy for her to respond to his tender expressions with affectionate glances of her own.

Once they got their dozen charges settled into the pew, instead of her sitting at one end and Chandler on the other as they normally did, he directed Bobby to replace Magdalene and seated her next to him.

Pastor Hall spoke with conviction. "Today I want to walk you through the Word and show you how much God loves you. In Isaiah, He promised a crown of beauty for the ashes of your life, a gladness to replace your mourning, praise in exchange for despair. He longs for each of us to be an oak of righteousness that we might display His splendor. As His bride, He sees you wearing a garment of salvation, a robe of righteousness, and adorned with jewels. You have no idea how beautiful we are to Him."

His words brought tears to Magdalene's eyes—no matter how men saw her or thought of her, she was beautiful to Christ.

"In Song of Solomon, the bridegroom refers to his bride as fairest among women, beautiful, the choice one. He states there is no spot in thee—meaning to Christ, you are flawless. We are His beloved bride, and He is completely taken with each of us.

"And turning to the King's marriage psalm, He states, 'so shall the king greatly desire thy beauty.' The King of kings and Lord of Lords desires your beauty! We are each beautiful to Him."

Magdalene rejoiced at his profound words. No one had ever desired her beauty before, and yet God did! She was beautiful to Him.

Magdalene felt lighter than she had in years. For the first time in her entire life, she actually felt beautiful. It didn't even matter that no one could see her beauty besides God. A smile settled on her lips, and she sensed an inner glow. *Thank You, Lord, for making me beautiful to You!*

After church, Chandler kept staring at her, almost as if he caught a glimpse of her beauty but couldn't quite figure out what had changed, yet knew something had. All the children napped on Sunday, so Chandler invited her for a walk after lunch. The seriousness of his expression caused trepidation to settle in the pit of her stomach. After the horrendous week she'd just survived, she wondered how much more either of them could withstand.

Chandler led her to the beach, keeping his promise not to touch her except for show when others were present. They settled in the sand, watching the waves come and go. For a long time, he said nothing and Magdalene began to relax, enjoying the sound of the water.

"Tomorrow, I'd like to take the children to Woodward's Gardens."

"Can we afford such an extravagance?"

"We'll have to. It will be our last day together, and I want the children to remember each other and the outing with fondness."

All the air left her lungs. What was he saying? Tears sprang to her eyes and she gasped for new air. Staring at him in unbelief, she saw tears in his eyes as well.

"Tuesday a new family will pick up Frankie, and by the end of the week, several other children may be gone as well."

The newspaper article. Her tears trailed down her cheeks,

dropping off her chin onto the skirt of her yellow dress. Would her mistake forever haunt them?

"You must hate me," she said in a tortured whisper.

His compassionate expression assured her that wasn't the case. "No, if anything, I hate myself for not being a wiser steward of what God gave me."

"Chandler, don't blame yourself. How could you have known?"

"I couldn't have known, but I should have hoped for the best and planned for the worst when Warren died."

A tear escaped his eye as well, but he quickly wiped it away.

"Bobby and Sarah?" She couldn't even give voice to the entire question.

"Maybe." He swallowed hard. "There's a request." His words were weighed down with pain.

"Couldn't we adopt them?" she asked, blinking furiously to prevent more tears from escaping and racing down her cheeks.

He gazed at her through red-rimmed, watery eyes. "I've thought about it, tried to convince myself keeping them is the right thing to do. But in my heart, Magdalene, I know I'm not being honest or honorable. We don't have a real marriage, and we can't offer them a mother and father who love each other." Tears now flowed freely down his face, and he no longer tried to hide them.

Magdalene laid her forehead against raised knees and sobbed. This was her fault. He'd offered her a real marriage, and her pride insisted she refuse. Now her pride was costing her all the people dearest to her heart.

&

Chandler fought the urge to pull her into his arms; instead he cried for the losses they faced. On the walk back to the orphanage, neither he nor Magdalene spoke, both bearing the weight of their grief alone.

Thinking back to the pastor's sermon that morning, he'd realized Magdalene was his beloved bride and he was completely taken with her. He loved her so much, it hurt. Knowing she felt little for him increased the pain.

Somehow they got through the rest of the day, maintaining as much normalcy as possible. At least they both managed not to cry in front of the children. Magdalene read to them from a book called *Anne* by Constance Fenimore Woolson, a newly-released novel following the life of an orphan.

After they tucked in the children and prayed with them, Chandler returned to his office to review the other applications. Moments after he settled in at his desk, Magdalene peeked in through the doorway.

"Good night, Chandler."

He smiled up at her, barely able to look at her now without being overcome by how precious she was to him. "Sleep well, my Maggie."

She smiled back. "You, too."

"In all honesty, I doubt either of us will."

A sad expression settled on her face. "I know."

The longing in her eyes nearly proved his undoing. He grabbed the sides of his chair in a stranglehold to force himself to remain seated. His heartbeat pounded in his ears.

Finally, she spoke, breaking the pull keeping their gazes interlocked. "I'll take the couch tonight."

"Please take the bed. I'll be here for several hours and don't want to disturb you."

"As you wish. See you tomorrow." She closed the door and was gone.

Chandler prayerfully read the applications, having difficulty concentrating. Some lines he read over at least ten times before his brain registered the words.

At eleven he gave up, climbing the stairs to check each child once more. When he reached Frankie's bed, the tears came unbidden. Kissing the boy's cheek, he ran his fingers through the clump of dark, silky hair poking out above the covers. *Thank You, Lord, for the days we've had with him. Please watch over him, keep him safe, and let his new family love him even more than Maggie and I do.*

Chandler left the children all sleeping soundly, made certain all the lights were off, and headed to his own cottage. Standing in the bedroom doorway, he debated whether or not to kiss Magdalene good night as he had the night before. He tiptoed in stocking feet around the bed to where she lay on her side, facing the window.

He knelt beside the bed and reached for the silken strands of hair draped across her cheek. *I love her.* The truth of those words still frightened and amazed him. He enjoyed the softness of her hair against his fingers. Placing a featherlight kiss on her cheek, he felt her even breathing against his face.

She stirred, opening her eyes. "Chandler." She whispered his name and a tiny smile touched her lips. Pulling her arm from under the covers, she gently stroked his whiskers, sending a shudder through him.

He didn't breathe, didn't move. His heart, however, suddenly jolted into overdrive. Mere inches separated their lips, and ever so slowly Magdalene closed the space. She kissed him long and slow. Had God answered his prayer for her to love him?

When she finally pulled back from him, she whispered, "I'm ready to be your wife—completely. I'm not afraid anymore."

Overwhelming joy flooded him; she finally loved him! He cupped his hand behind her head, drawing her to him once again. This time he kissed her with unbridled passion, but through the haze of their ardor, the truth came unwelcome and unwanted. He abruptly ended the kiss and rested his forehead on the edge of the bed. Breathless, he silently cried out to God for the strength to do the right thing.

Her fingers tangled in his hair. "Chandler?"

He stood, needing to put some distance between them. "This isn't right, Magdalene." Her eyes misted over, and she dropped her chin to her chest so he could no longer see her expression. "You're only doing this because of our conversation earlier today at the beach."

She didn't deny it; in fact, she said nothing at all, but her shoulders quaked from her silent sobs.

Having regained control, he sat on the side of the bed and took her hand in his. "Maggie, if we do this without love, you'll grow to hate me someday. You said so yourself, just the night before last."

She agreed in a barely perceivable nod.

If only she knew what this decision cost him. He desired nothing more than for them to become one flesh, not for Bobby and Sarah, but because she truly loved him and wanted to be his real wife. He loved her so much that he wasn't willing to settle for less from her.

He lifted her chin and wiped the tears from her cheeks with his thumbs. "I love you for being willing to sacrifice your hopes and dreams for them."

Magdalene knew he did love her the same way he loved each of the orphans, but not the way she loved him, not the way a man loves a woman.

He wrapped her in gentle arms, and she laid her head on his shoulder. Rocking her back and forth, he ran his hand over the length of her hair. "I like your hair down."

"But it's so wild and bushy."

"I like it that way."

"Thank you." She pulled back from him. "We'd better get

some sleep. Dawn isn't very far off."

He kissed her cheek, pushed her back against the pillows, and pulled the covers tightly around her. "Good night, Magdalene."

When the door clicked shut, she whispered, "Good night, Chandler. I love you."

Magdalene spent the rest of the night fighting off feelings of rejection. Chandler's excuse sounded plausible, but the truth was, he didn't *want* her. Her face burned just thinking about how forward she'd been, throwing herself at him with reckless abandon. What had she been thinking? At least he'd been kind in his refusal.

Once the hustle and bustle of the day began, she had little time to dwell on such nonsense. She did, however, avoid eye contact at the breakfast table, mortified by her behavior.

Soon after breakfast, they loaded the children into the buckboard for their outing. "Have you visited Woodward's Gardens before?" Chandler asked Magdalene once they were all situated and headed toward town.

"Not for years. The last time I went was with Gabrielle, Nathaniel, and Isabel, before they were even married and Izzy was just about ten."

They shared small talk in between games and songs with the children.

Chandler paid $3.50 for their group's admission. "Where should we start?"

"The animals," Bobby answered.

"Yeah, the animals," all the children chimed in unison.

Chandler smiled at Magdalene. "The animals it is."

Leading them through the tunnel under Fourteenth Street, Chandler said, "I always liked the animals best, too. My mother brought me here often as a child. I was ten or eleven when it opened."

First they came upon the large bear pit, watching a baby bear dance around his mama. The children giggled and imitated him.

"Uncle Chandler, when are you and Miss Maggie going to have a baby?" Sarah asked.

He grinned at her, and Magdalene felt her cheeks grow hot. The thought of carrying Chandler's child brought a rush of maternal desires.

"We have all of you, Sarah, and for now, that's enough. Let's move on to the camel yards."

Magdalene wondered when it would no longer be enough. When would Chandler desire a real wife, one he loved? *Stop it! One day at a time is all we have to get through.*

The children were noisy, making animal sounds and laughing, and Magdalene loved every moment with them. They enjoyed watching the buffalo and deer. Then they moved on to the outdoor gymnasium for the children to run and play. She and Chandler settled on a bench to watch.

A familiar form caught her eye. Magdalene froze. Isabel. She hadn't seen her sister since the wedding three days before. She had no desire to see her now or for Chandler to see her, either. He didn't need the reminder of what he'd given up.

Wait. A man took her hand! Who? He looked familiar. Magdalene stared, searching to remember. . . . "Sam Starr!"

"What?" Chandler appeared truly puzzled.

She hadn't realized she'd spoken aloud. Now, she'd have to explain. How would he feel, seeing Isabel with another?

"Look over there." She pointed at the laughing couple. "Isabel is here with the reporter." Her heart dropped to her feet. *What if she tells him all the things she and Josephine were discussing a few days ago?* Magdalene couldn't bear the thought of her private pain splashed across the San Francisco newspaper.

Chandler pulled his shirt collar away from his neck, a frown drawing his brows together and his eyes never leaving Isabel.

"What if she tells him about our marriage? What if he prints—"

"Magdalene, excuse me a moment." Chandler rose and walked toward them.

She watched through misty eyes as Chandler greeted the surprised couple. Sam Starr smiled and shook his hand, acting as if they were old and dear friends. Isabel looked uncomfortable but waved when Chandler pointed her out on the bench. Sam said something and moved toward her; meanwhile Chandler spoke to Isabel alone. Their heads were bent slightly and close together, and his back was to Magdalene. Jealousy filled her entire being.

"Mrs. Alexandre, I wanted to congratulate you on your marriage and apologize for making more out of your letter than I should have." Mr. Starr settled on the bench beside her.

Magdalene tore her gaze from Chandler and Isabel to focus on Mr. Starr. "Thank you."

"Your sister is quite the girl."

"Charming and witty—that's Isabel." Bitterness wove itself through her words. She'd heard them her whole life and was sick to death of Isabel and her appeal, especially at this moment when she worked at beguiling Magdalene's husband.

Mr. Starr stood. "Well, I should get back to her. Good day, Mrs. Alexandre." He touched the brim of his bowler.

"Good day, Mr. Starr."

Magdalene disliked herself for being curt and for all these hateful feelings toward her sister, but most of all she abhorred the fact that she couldn't win the heart of the man she loved.

twelve

Chandler left Isabel with a veiled threat. "If I read anything about me, Magdalene, or our marriage in the newspaper, you'll have me to answer to. Understood?"

She nodded, and he strode away from her, back toward his bride. Thank God he had never seriously considered Isabel as a contender. He didn't like the spoiled child she turned out to be, not one bit.

Sam stopped in front of him. "Our agreement still stands. Just because I'm courting Isabel doesn't mean I'll break my word to you, no matter what she may disclose."

"I appreciate knowing that. Thank you." He shook his hand again and strode back to his spot on the bench. "Fancy meeting them here. I had no idea they were courting."

"Nor did I."

Magdalene's frosty words matched the cold shoulder she bestowed on him. Next, they visited the marine aquarium, the largest in the country housing both salt and freshwater tanks. Chandler admired the large photographs of California scenery lining the walls, but he couldn't draw Magdalene's interest. They also toured the museum, conservatories, and small, but select, art gallery. He and the children conversed throughout the day, but Magdalene remained stone-faced and silent. He figured knowing what lay ahead tonight dampened her mood—either that or something having to do with Isabel.

"Magdalene, I plan to tell the children about Frankie as soon as we finish supper," Chandler informed her as they gathered around the table. "I know this is difficult, but for his sake, could you please liven up?"

She nodded but looked as if she might cry.

After he said grace, Mrs. Lindsay served chicken and dumplings, one of Frankie's favorite meals. Afterward, she carried out a chocolate layer cake with candles. All the children reacted with chatter and excitement.

"Yes, Children, it's a party!" He spoke loud enough to be heard above all of them. A dozen pair of eyes focused on him, and he forced himself to appear jubilant—a difficult task, considering the sizable ache in his heart. "Tonight is a special celebration. We're having an adoption party!"

" 'Doption? What's that?" Frankie asked. Since he was the youngest, not quite three, he hadn't had adoption explained to him yet.

"An adoption is when a real family with a mother and a father decides to invite one of you children to come and live with them and become their very own family member." Despite his excited and upbeat tone, their little faces appeared crestfallen.

"Can you imagine how wonderful to have your own mother and father, maybe some sisters and brothers?" Magdalene chimed in.

"A house with your own room?" he added.

"I'd be scared," Sarah said, her eyes large.

"Who's being adopted?" Bobby asked. The look on his face clearly revealed he hoped it wasn't him.

Chandler glanced at Magdalene for support. "Frankie."

The other eleven orphans appeared relieved, but Frankie started to cry.

Chandler rushed to Frankie's chair and swept him into his arms. "It's okay, little fellow," he promised, kissing his forehead.

Magdalene took Frankie's hand. "Look at your cake! Let's light those candles so you can blow them out!"

The child nodded but looked fearful. Chandler passed Frankie to Magdalene while he lit the candles. Then he lifted him near the cake, and Frankie blew and blew. The children laughed at his antics, and when all the candles were finally extinguished, Magdalene cut fifteen slices.

Chandler held Frankie on his lap while they both ate their cake. Frankie had chocolate all over his face, hands, and Chandler. The cake certainly lightened the mood. When the chocolate mess was finally cleaned up, all the children were in good humor and acting silly.

Chandler led his crew into the parlor, keeping Frankie on his lap. Tonight he spoke on God's plan for families, sharing with them what God said about mothers, fathers, and little children. He also told them how much Jesus loves people, especially children.

Then instead of reading, Magdalene told a made-up story about a boy named Frankie, who didn't have a mother or father, and a couple named Farnsworth who had no children but wanted some really badly. They searched high and low for a special child, and finally they found Frankie.

Chandler was glad he'd stayed for story hour. His motive had been purely selfish; he wasn't ready to put Frankie down yet. Magdalene mesmerized all of them with her yarn. He saw each of their faces relax as she presented adoption in such a positive light.

"They founded me?" Frankie asked.

"Yes." Chandler tweaked Frankie's nose. "They found very special you." He hugged the child tight, swallowing the lump he'd been fighting all evening.

"Bath time! Tonight is Sarah, Susie, and Frankie."

Magdalene reached for Frankie, but he tightened his hold on Chandler's neck.

"You do it." Frankie pointed at Chandler.

"Me? I don't think I know how."

"Miss Maggie will help."

Chandler helped Frankie pack his few belongings while Magdalene assisted Sarah and Susie with their baths. With Frankie, she instructed Chandler in the fine art of child bathing. He ended up almost as wet as Frankie, and bathing a child with her produced a longing in his heart for them to be a real family. He could imagine them together, bathing their tiny babe. He closed his eyes, fighting off double sorrow—sorrow at losing Frankie and sorrow for the children they might never have.

After all the children were tucked in and prayed for, he and Magdalene knelt beside Frankie's bed and prayed for him and his future family.

"Miss Maggie, will you wock me?"

Magdalene lifted the child and carried him to the rocker.

Chandler kissed the top of each of their heads and left. He needed air. He took the stairs two at a time, and tears began to trickle down his face before he even reached the door. Outside Chandler looked up into the starry sky, longing to cry out his agony to God, but no words came—only more tears. He and Magdalene were people living out the consequences of their own bad choices.

❧

Magdalene held Frankie snugly against her, and they rocked and rocked. She prayed for him and his parents to love each other quickly, and she begged God not to find homes for any more of their orphans.

She had no idea how long she rocked. Mrs. Lindsay had

retired ages ago, but Magdalene couldn't bring herself to end her final time with Frankie.

Finally Chandler came back upstairs. He knelt beside the rocker and looked exhausted. He'd been crying, and even though she didn't want to care, she did. Her heart ached for him—for them.

"Maggie, it's after midnight. Why don't you come to bed?"

At her nod, he lifted Frankie from her arms and laid him on his bed. Together they tucked him in and each gave him one last good-night kiss. Then Chandler took her hand and led her to the little cottage they shared. Once inside, he pulled her into his arms and held her tight for a moment. After kissing her temple, he released her completely, and she immediately missed his closeness.

" 'Night, Maggie," he whispered, guiding her into the bedroom they didn't share. He closed the door between them before she could offer to take the couch. Magdalene spent a fitful night trying to sleep and forget the image of Chandler and Isabel with their heads close together in intimate conversation. Just thinking about it caused her stomach to ache.

❧

Chandler thought he'd heard Magdalene crying in the night, but he didn't dare go check on her. Each time he held her, he just wanted to hold her more. He ran his hand across his jaw and sighed. Where did they go from here?

After breakfast, he and Frankie left for town to meet his new parents. Chandler figured this way would be easier on everyone. He assured the little boy that Miss Maggie's and the other children's tears weren't because adoption was a sad thing, but because they all loved him so much and would miss him terribly. Frankie seemed to accept Chandler's explanation.

The transition went better than he'd hoped. The Farnsworths were kind, loving people. Answering the door with a puppy for Frankie was ingenious, and he didn't even cry when Chandler hugged him good-bye because of his excitement over the dog. Chandler didn't cry either, at least not until their front door closed and no one could witness his sobbing.

Chandler decided to pay his mother a visit before he picked up their mail and a few supplies. Baldwin escorted him into her sitting room, and she came in a few moments later. Rising, he placed a kiss on each of her cheeks.

"I've missed you. How are the newlyweds?" She sat on the small sofa and straightened her skirts.

Chandler had no desire to discuss private matters with his mother. "Fine. I came by to see if Father saw Sam Starr's retraction in the newspaper."

"Yes, and he felt satisfied—though he'd have preferred it never happened."

Chandler sighed. "Me, too. Will we ever have an amicable relationship?"

"Frankly, that's up to the two of you. I cannot predict how either of you will behave. I do, however, know your father has few regrets in his life; but of those few, you are by far the largest and heaviest."

"Why doesn't he change, then, treat me differently?" Chandler exhaled a frustrated sigh.

"He wonders the same about you. The truth is, change is hard and old habits die a slow death. You both have bad habits in the way you treat one another. Do you remember the story of your father and me, as newlyweds, leaving France and our families to find the American dream?" Her eyes took on a faraway look.

Chandler nodded and his mother continued. "What we never mentioned was, we left without either family's blessing. We sailed to America in pursuit of wealth and opportunity, leaving behind hurt and angry parents who didn't understand. Looking back, we were foolish, but then leaving seemed cosmopolitan—the thing to do.

"Through letters, my parents and I reconciled. Your father reestablished a relationship with his mother but never with his father. When your grandfather died, Archard never forgave himself for the rift between them. Now he faces a similar rift with his youngest son and would give his right arm for a second chance."

"He's the one who despised me even when I was a child." The old hurt returned.

"I've only recently realized he despised the illness that held you captive, not you." She cocked her head slightly and sent him a smile of understanding.

"As a young boy, how was I to know the difference?" His choked voice echoed the deep pain he carried within.

"You couldn't, and he was wrong. But then you walked away from him and the family business to find your own way."

"To escape his displeasure."

"And you replaced him with a surrogate father. That hurt him deeply, Chandler." His mother reached over and patted his hand.

"It wasn't intentional. I ached for a father—someone who'd love me with no demands or expectations—and Mr. Baxter willingly filled the role."

"He was a good man, your Mr. Baxter. I'm only sorry your father never realized it. He only saw him as a thief who stole his son's affection. Now that he's gone, Archard hopes to win back your love and respect, but he doesn't know how. He believes if you came to work for him, you'd get to know him and recognize that he's not such a bad person."

Choked up by his mother's revelations, Chandler had no answers. He paced the floor. God had brought him to a point where he desired healing with his father, but how? "I'll work hard to build a solid relationship with him. I'll ask God to help me forgive him for past hurts and love him the way I did Mr. Baxter. I'll ask the Lord to make me the son He'd have me be."

His mother quickly wiped the drizzle of tears from her cheeks. Polite society did not cry publicly, even if the only public around was her son.

Chandler felt grateful Warren had taught him to feel and express those feelings.

"One problem solved," his mother said. "Shall we move on to the next?"

"What next problem?" He returned to his chair, sensing his mother referred to Magdalene.

"Your wife. I assume the marriage isn't going well, is it?"

"Why would you assume that?" He squirmed under his mother's astute gaze.

"You may fool some of the people, some of the time, but you are not fooling your own mother. You look awful, and the bags under your eyes tell me you're not sleeping well."

"I'm a newlywed. Newlyweds aren't supposed to sleep well." He hoped his joke would provide a diversion.

No luck. His mother was like a bulldog when she got hold of something. "I noticed the way you gazed at Magdalene and heard the defensiveness in your voice when your father referred to her as a homely spinster."

"You don't think she's homely, do you?"

"No, I don't. On your wedding day, she was quite lovely."

"And what do you mean, 'the way I gazed at her'?"

Chandler studied his mother.

"You're in love with her. My guess, based on your appearance, is that the feelings aren't mutual."

Thinking of Magdalene brought a slight smile to his lips. "I do love her—so much." He shook his head, puzzled as to how to win her love.

"Be patient and woo her." She smiled, obviously pleased with the way their conversation had gone.

"She's so distant, I don't even know where or how to begin."

"Sounds like the same problem your father had with you."

The irony of her observation caught his attention. "*As a man measures it out, so it is measured back to him.*" "You're right, it does. Where does one begin to repair and rebuild a relationship?"

"I think time and talking—"

"Speaking of time," Chandler glanced at his pocket watch, "I have several stops before I can head home. Can we continue this soon?" He placed another kiss on her cheek.

"I love you, Son. Your God will guide you to the correct answers with both your father and Magdalene."

Yes, my God will. I'm glad you recognize the truth of your statement.

They hugged and she escorted him to the front door. "Don't make plans on New Year's Eve. I have a surprise for you and your new bride."

"Not a levee." Leave it to his mother to plan a big reception. "Things are bad enough. I don't think a party in honor of our marriage will help."

"Every wife deserves a celebration and gifts. Don't worry. Everything will work out fine."

"I sure hope you're right. Bye, Mother."

On his way to the general store, Chandler prayed. *Please make things right between Magdalene and me. Give her a forgiving heart. And then, Lord, I need to make things right with my father as well. He's old and may not be around much longer, but there's so much pain between us. Show me how to make amends for the years of pain we've caused each other.*

Chandler thought about what his mother had said. Maybe his father hadn't meant to hurt him. Maybe he'd truly been pained by Chandler's thin, sickly body. Maybe he'd avoided him, not because of disgust, but guilt. A new understanding dawned.

When he arrived back at the orphanage, Chandler went to his office to go through the mail and hopefully get a little bookwork done before supper. Another letter from New York was in the pile. He opened it first.

> *Dear Mr. Alexandre:*
> *This letter is to inform you as of January 1, 1883, the estate of Warren Baxter will again be contributing funds to the San Francisco Christian Home for Orphans and Foundlings. We will be donating the same amount as before, so you may continue the work so dear to Mr. Baxter's heart.*

Chandler went limp in his chair. He reread the first paragraph again, but the words didn't change. This meant his marriage to Magdalene was no longer necessary. Instead of joy over the news, sadness spread through his entire being. Chandler finished the rest of the letter.

> *Upon reading Mr. Baxter's journals, his nephew, who now controls the funds, discovered the orphanage was his uncle's dearest loved*

endeavor and most important project. I'm certain
you can appreciate his desire to use the money in
ways most pleasing to his uncle. We do, however,
wish to apologize for any minor problems the
young Mr. Baxter may have caused during our
brief lapse with the endowment.

Respectfully,
Winston Wallace Williams III

With the bold script, Chandler's future appeared bleak. They had the nerve to refer to minor problems. If they only knew the havoc they'd triggered in his life in the past two weeks—in all their lives.

"What now, Lord? What do I do?"

Chandler tucked the letter under some other paperwork. He needed to think and pray.

thirteen

Magdalene grew more bitter and angry as the days passed.
Two weeks had elapsed since their wedding day, and she
avoided Chandler whenever possible, often disliking him
with as much intensity as she loved him. Why did he have to
care more for Isabel? With each trip he made into town, she
wondered if they had a secret rendezvous and laughed at her
supposed stupidity.

He'd taken to sleeping in his office, so they no longer saw
much of each other—just at mealtime. She found excuses not
to join them for his Bible teaching anymore. The hardest part
was, she sensed God's displeasure, and He felt very far away.

The whole marriage plan had backfired. She now knew
they'd made a huge mistake, but there was no way out.
They'd lost Frankie ten days ago and four other boys since.
Somehow, Chandler had managed to keep Bobby and Sarah,
but she wondered for how much longer. Christmas lurked
only five days away, and she must start making preparations.

Today she'd convinced Mrs. Lindsay to let her and the children have the kitchen. They'd bake and decorate gingerbread
men. She hoped Chandler planned to get a tree soon. No matter what their feelings were for one another, they needed to
make the holidays special for the children, especially since no
one knew how long any of them would be there.

Magdalene rounded up the seven children. She got out
bowls and ingredients. She assigned each child a duty to help
complete the process. They measured, mixed, rolled, cut, and

baked. Flour covered the kitchen from one end to the other. As soon as the cookies came out of the oven, Bobby punched a hole in the top of each cookie so it could be hung from string to decorate the tree.

"Smells like heaven in here." Chandler entered the kitchen just as they finished their cookies. "I have a surprise—come see."

All the children rushed out the door, and Magdalene went to the window to peek at what all the fuss was about. "The tree! He got the tree."

Chandler dragged the Christmas tree into the parlor, the children on his heels.

Feeling restless and not wanting to spend the afternoon with him, Magdalene formed a plan. Once the tree stood straight and tall in the corner, she approached him. "Would you mind if I went to the city?"

He glanced from the tree to her, his expression startled. "Why—if you don't mind my asking?"

"Since Christmas is so close, I wish to shop for a few gifts for the children."

"We could decorate this afternoon—all of us together, and I could take you to town tomorrow."

The way a happy family would do things. "I was hoping you'd allow me to take the buggy myself, so I could spend time with my family." Magdalene focused on the window, avoiding his disappointed look. "I miss them very much. I'll return by late tomorrow afternoon."

Chandler sighed. "If that's what you want. Shall the children and I wait until you get back to trim the tree?"

"That's not necessary. They'd be disappointed if you asked them to wait."

Chandler studied the excited children and nodded. "I'll

prepare the buggy for your departure."

❧

Chandler left the house with an ache the size of California in his heart. "Why, Lord? Why can't I reach her?" With each day, Magdalene slipped farther away.

Entering the barn, he groomed the two horses, harnessed them, and hitched them to the buggy. He thought over the past two weeks. If any marriage was doomed, theirs appeared to be. He led the horses to the front of the orphanage where Magdalene impatiently waited. He wondered if she'd ever come back.

She patted Stubby's neck. "Thank you for getting them ready."

He nodded. "Will your dad or Nathaniel be available to help you with them tonight and tomorrow?"

"Believe it or not, I can hitch up a wagon all by myself." The way she looked at him—almost a glare—caused him to realize how intensely she disliked him.

"Magdalene—don't leave like this." He placed a re-straining hand on her arm, but she jerked away.

"Like what?"

"Why are you so angry? Why do you hate me?"

"I'm not angry, Chandler—just resigned." She bowed her head.

"Resigned to what? Making us both miserable?" He ran a frustrated hand over the stubble of whiskers on his jaw.

She climbed up into the two-seater buggy. "Resigned to the misery of being your wife." Taking the reins, she flicked them across the horses' hindquarters and the buggy lurched forward.

Sorrow nearly choked him. She was miserable, and he knew what he had to do—the very thing he'd avoided the past ten days. While the children were having dinner inside with Mrs. Lindsay, he went into his office, quietly closing the door behind him. Pulling the correct law book off the shelf, he found the law he'd put off reading for over a week.

Annul. Different from divorce in that divorce ends a valid marriage. Annulment ends an invalid or illegal marriage.

Chandler would never consider divorce—not ever. God frowned on such an action, but perhaps an annulment would be okay. After all, they'd never consummated their relationship. Though theirs wasn't an illegal marriage, it certainly seemed invalid. He'd have to check into that avenue.

He laid his head on his desk. "Lord, this isn't my choice, but maybe You restored the funding so I could release her. She hates me. I've tried to reach her, but she shuts me out. Please show me the right thing."

After a knock on his office door, Mrs. Lindsay entered carrying a bowl of beef stew and some fresh bread. "You don't need to be missing meals. You'll be needin' your strength to decorate this old house for the holidays."

She placed the food on his desk in front of him, and he knew her observant eyes didn't miss the fact he'd been crying.

"I been prayin' for you and the missus."

"Thank you."

She nodded and left him alone.

After forcing himself to eat, Chandler rounded up the children. They spent the rest of the day stringing popcorn, hanging fresh pine boughs, and decorating with gingerbread men. By nightfall, the place looked pretty good. He hoped Magdalene would be pleased.

Thoughts of her were always followed by a heaviness in his heart. What had happened? Somehow, he'd failed her and failed God.

The only bright spot in his life these days were the tiny improvements in his relationship with his father. He'd been going home three days a week to spend time with him and seek his advice on business wisdom with the orphanage. His father enjoyed being needed and sought out. Chandler hoped one day soon they could move their conversations into more personal realms.

⁊

Magdalene's heart felt like a chunk of stone in her chest. So much hate, anger, and bitterness resided inside her. She wished for the release of tears, but just as feeling had become impossible for her, so had crying.

She directed the buggy straight to Gabrielle's, having no energy to shop for the children. Perhaps after some time with her older sister and a good night's rest, she'd be ready to face the prospect of gift buying tomorrow.

Magdalene tied the horses to the hitching rail and trudged the rest of the way up the hill. A tired but smiling Gabrielle greeted her from the rocker on the porch.

"Magdalene! What a nice surprise. I just laid the children down for a nap and thought I'd enjoy some fresh air and tea." She set her cup down and rose to hug her sister.

Magdalene fell into Gabby's arms, and the tears she'd wished for suddenly flowed like a raging river. Gabrielle embraced her, letting her cry. Finally she directed her to the porch swing, and Magdalene continued to sob on Gabrielle's shoulder.

Spent, Magdalene lifted her head. "Thank you. I just needed someone to hold me."

"What about Chandler?"

"He's in love with Isabel, not me."

"What?" Gabrielle's eyes grew large and doubt-filled.

Magdalene nodded and whispered, "It's true."

"Start at the beginning and tell me everything," Gabrielle said, pushing Magdalene's hair back out of her face. "I find this really hard to believe."

In a flat, quiet tone, Magdalene said, "I overheard Isabel and Chandler's niece, Josephine, at our wedding. She said something to the effect that Chandler struggled to decide between the two of us but ended up choosing me because of the children. He's selfless, so it makes perfect sense he'd settle on who's best for them over what his heart desired."

"Magdalene, for whatever reason, he *did* choose you. You're his wife." Gabrielle's words held compassion, yet a certain firmness.

"Not really." *Only by law, but not in any other way.*

"Yes, you really are. I was there, remember? I witnessed it happening."

Dare she tell the most intimate details of their relationship? Magdalene wandered across the porch and returned to stand before Gabrielle. "We've never. . ."

Gabrielle's mouth fell open. "Not once?"

Magdalene shook her head. Embarrassed, she turned to face the bay. "He wanted to that first night. . . ."

"You denied your own husband?" Gabrielle sounded astounded.

Magdalene turned back to face her sister. "I wasn't prepared for it to happen. In all honesty, the idea barely occurred to me. I didn't think he'd want to—I mean, at least not with me. He's not attracted to me or in love me, so why would he want to. . . you know?"

"You, my dear sister, have a lot to learn about men."

"I'm sure you're right. After much prayer and thought, I offered myself to him a couple of nights later—" Her voice cracked with a sob. "He—didn't—want me."

Gabrielle stood and wrapped Magdalene in another hug. "Did he say that?"

"No." She sniffed. "He said he wanted to wait until I was more sure of my feelings. He didn't want me to come to him out of obligation."

Gabrielle pulled back to look into Magdalene's eyes. "Now that sounds like Chandler. He's an honorable man."

"I know, but I think he regrets yoking himself to me. We saw Isabel at Woodward's Gardens, and he excused himself and rushed to her side. They stood huddled together, sharing intimate conversation, while her beau came over to speak to me. Why, she never even spoke to me—only waved from afar, and do you know why?"

Gabrielle shook her head.

"Guilt. How does one face her sister when she's pursuing her sister's husband?"

"Magdalene, you're basing all this on supposition, not fact. Isabel is sparking with that newspaper fellow." Gabrielle's voice had grown slightly impatient.

"I know, but it's Chandler she really wants. I heard her say so to his niece. She's set her cap for him, have no doubt about that. And now all of a sudden, he's been making trips to town every couple of days. He's never done that before in all the three years I've known him. Seems to me, he's meeting some-one—and that someone is Isabel."

Gabrielle's face went white, and she shook her head.

"What?" Magdalene demanded, sensing Gabrielle had information she withheld. "You know something. Tell me!"

"I'm sure there's an explanation." Gabrielle rubbed her forehead between her eyes as if she'd suddenly developed a headache.

"Explanation for what?"

Gabrielle sighed. "I saw Chandler and Isabel together a couple of weeks ago. I thought nothing of it, just as I'd think nothing of you being in town with Nathaniel."

Magdalene felt as if she'd been punched in the gut. She grabbed hold of the balcony railing to steady herself. "When? Where?" She didn't desire to know, yet had to know at the same time.

"A few days after your wedding. They were walking together down Market Street. Nathaniel waved, but they didn't see us."

Probably too wrapped up in each other. "Were they close— touching?" Her stomach clenched with the pain of certainty. It was one thing to suspect, but quite another to know for sure.

"Of course not! Magdalene, your mind is running away with you." Concern lined Gabrielle's face.

"Tell me exactly what you saw—everything."

"Nathaniel and I left the children with Mother, so we could talk about our Christmas plans for this year. We were in the buggy, returning home, when he pointed them out. They were on the opposite side of the street, and though we waved and called to them, neither heard or saw us."

"What were they doing?"

"Laughing and walking. Chandler carried several packages, so I figured he asked Isabel to help him pick out a Christmas gift for you."

It sounded plausible, and she so wanted to believe Gabrielle's explanation. She dropped down into the rocker. "Is that what you really think?"

"Yes, yes it is. Chandler Alexandre is a man of integrity, and I don't believe he'd dishonor your wedding vows. You two must talk and resolve some of these issues. There are too many questions. Ask him!"

"I'm afraid. What if his answer is what I suspect?" She gripped the arms on the rocker, wondering if not knowing was easier.

"Then God will give you the grace you need. You can't fight a war unless you know where the enemy is, but I think the battleground is in your mind. You've allowed your imagination to run away with you. Take captive your thoughts, Magdalene. Don't think about things that aren't absolutely one hundred percent truth."

"So you think I should give him the benefit of the doubt and go home and ask?"

"Yes. Love believes, hopes, and trusts."

Magdalene had never felt so confused. She could convince herself to believe either way. She did need to talk this out with Chandler, because their problems were taking a great toll on her relationship with God.

"If you want, we can go ask Isabel."

Just hearing her name brought a stab of jealousy to Magdalene's heart. "No, I'd rather ask Chandler." *At least he won't gloat.*

"And Magdalene. . ." Settling back into the porch swing, Gabrielle sounded unsure whether she should continue or not.

"What?"

"The apostle Paul says it's not a good idea for a wife to leave her husband's physical needs unmet and vice versa. You leave him vulnerable to temptation."

"So, if he is seeing Isabel, it's my fault?"

"No, and don't be so defensive. I'm just saying you not only need to talk, you need to. . .become his wife." A baby cried from inside the house. "One of the girls is awake."

Gabrielle left her alone on the porch. "I tried," Magdalene whispered. "He doesn't want me."

fourteen

Magdalene slept better than she had since she'd gotten married. Opening her eyes to the morning light, she actually felt refreshed. Retiring to bed alone every night, as a married woman, had made sleeping difficult because of the guilt and rejection issues.

Stretching, she enjoyed the precious sound of her sleeping nieces and nephews. After her conversation with Gabrielle, she walked along the bay and had a long talk with God, which included a lot of repentance. She was now prepared to go home, open up to Chandler, and work at being the wife God desired her to be.

After breakfast, Magdalene bid her sister, Nathaniel, and the children good-bye. She hitched up the buggy—by herself—and aimed the horses toward town. She anticipated finding a small gift for each of the children but had no idea what to get for Chandler.

After a successful morning in town, Magdalene headed home, actually looking forward to being there. Chandler came out and met her. She wondered if he'd been watching for her.

With the bitterness gone and renewed hope, seeing him caused her stomach to do a somersault. He appeared relieved to see her as well. Lifting her down from the buggy, he whispered, "I missed you." He took her hands in his own. The action nearly undid her. His thumbs gently drew circles across her fingers. She focused on the ground beneath her feet, afraid if she looked into his eyes, her every feeling would pour forth in bold proclamation.

Taking their intertwined hands, he moved them to her chin, lifting it until their eyes met. He lowered her hands to her sides and slipped his free, placing them on her shoulders. He drew her toward him while, inch by inch, his lips moved closer to hers. What in the world was a girl to do?

It ended up she did nothing at all except willingly let him kiss her. Unbeknownst to her before that moment, her lips had a mind of their own and savored the joy of his mouth on hers. When he pulled back, Magdalene lowered her lashes. Breathless, she rested her forehead against his chest.

❧

Chandler longed to see her eyes, read her expression. His mother said woo, and woo he would. He'd try one last time to win her heart before he offered her an annulment, and if he couldn't say the words "I love you" aloud because she wasn't ready to hear them, then he'd show her in every way he could. Did she understand his secret message hidden within the kiss, the message of commitment and forever?

Not wanting to rush her or scare her, he waited for her to make the next move. For several minutes, she stood with her head against his chest and his arms around her. Was she realizing this was where she belonged, wrapped in his embrace? *Dear Lord, please let her feel all the emotions I'm feeling. Open her heart and fill it with love for me.*

"Chandler, I'm sorry."

"Me too, Maggie." He kissed the top of her head. "Me too."

"I haven't been very nice."

"Nor have I."

She pulled free and put a few steps between them. Keeping her back to him, she said, "It's hard, knowing you'd have never married me if you hadn't had to."

Turning her around, he said, "I didn't have to marry you. I *chose* to marry you. There's a big difference."

Looking straight into his eyes, she said, "The truth is, Chandler, had you never received the letter that put the orphanage in an ominous financial position and had you not had an inheritance available to you should you ever marry, I'd still be Miss Fairchild—the woman you barely knew."

The pain in her eyes caused an ache in his heart. "I barely knew you because you shut me out. I tried to get to know you, but you insisted on distance between us."

"I didn't want you to hurt me then, and I still don't."

"Magdalene, I love you!" There—he'd said the words aloud. "Maybe we wouldn't have ever realized we were meant to be together if God hadn't put us in a situation where we had no choice. Can't you get past that and just accept where we are now?"

"If you love me, why are you suddenly going to town so often?"

Where did that come from? Chandler reached for her, and she willingly let him hold her. "I've been meeting with my father for the last couple of weeks. I'm working at reconciliation and picking information from his brilliant business mind at the same time."

She pulled back, peering deep into his eyes. "That's all?"

"What are you getting at?"

"Gabrielle saw you and Isabel together. Chandler, if you love her—if you realized she's really the one—"

"No!" He put distance between them. *She doesn't trust me! She thinks I'm dallying with Isabel behind her back.*

Lifting his hands in disgusted resignation, he turned back to face her. Hurt echoed through him. "I can't believe that after three years, you don't know me any better than that. I'm nothing if not honest."

Magdalene raised her chin. "Then why were you with her?"

"I'm not at liberty to say." He clenched his jaw. She'd not pry this out of him.

"How can we work on a real marriage if you keep secrets?" She stomped toward the house, and he led the horses into the barn.

"How, indeed?" It seemed every time they took one step forward, they fell back two. Was there really any hope for them, or were their lives destined to be a web of misunderstanding? He took deep, controlled breaths, trying to expel his anger.

≈

"I don't understand him," Magdalene grumbled on her way up the hill to the cottage. "If he has nothing to hide, why doesn't he tell me why they were together?"

Needing time to calm down before she greeted the children, Magdalene quietly snuck into the cottage. "He said he loved me." She spoke to her reflection in the mirror. "Why can't I believe him?" *Because men like Chandler Alexandre don't love women like me.* She curled up on the bed in a ball of misery.

Chandler's steps resounded across the wooden cottage porch. Magdalene sat up, not wishing to be found in such a pathetic state. She held her breath, hoping he'd assume she'd gone to the orphanage instead. Maybe he'd not check the bedroom.

No such luck. He stormed into the room, grabbed her by the arm, and dragged her behind him back down the hill and into the barn.

"You unhand me! What do you think you're doing?" Her

heart pounded, partially from anger and partially from fear. She'd never seen him like this before.

He led her to a bale of hay. "Sit down. You want to know what's between me and Isabel?" After pulling an old trunk from behind the grain bin, he snapped it open. "This! And this is all that's ever been between us." He pulled out a beautiful, red velvet dress and shoved it at her. Then he proceeded to pull out two smaller ones about Sarah's and Susie's sizes. "Hannah's and Rachel's will be finished day after tomorrow."

Magdalene hung her head. "I'm sorry I doubted you."

"Since I know nothing about sewing, I asked Isabel to come with me to make the purchase. I bought a length of red velvet, and she picked out all the other necessities."

Magdalene rose, carefully draping the new dress over her arm. "The dress is beautiful. I'm sorry I spoiled your surprise."

"I couldn't bring myself to let you doubt me for three more days just so you'd be surprised on Christmas morning." He took the dress from her and returned it to the trunk with the other two. Then he guided her back to the hay bale, squatting down in front of her. "I wish for our marriage to work. Can we put all the confusion and questions behind us and try?"

She touched his face. "Yes." He turned his head and kissed her palm.

Rising, he pulled her up with him. "Here's to a fresh start." He pulled her into his arms and kissed her until liquid fire ran through her veins.

The dinner bell sounded, startling them both. He held her face between his hands, laughing. "You, my dear wife, look completely disheveled and thoroughly kissed."

She mussed his hair and ran for the orphanage. Not quite to the porch, he caught up to her, grabbed her around the waist, and lifted her off the ground. He drizzled a fistful of straw over her hair. Wrestling with him for the rest of the straw, she tripped. They both toppled to the ground, where they stayed, laughing.

"Well it's about time you two started actin' like newly-weds." Magdalene's cheeks warmed at Mrs. Lindsay's declaration, and to make things worse, Chandler kissed her again right there in front of Mrs. Lindsay and seven giggling children who piled on top of them.

❧

Shortly before sunrise on Christmas morning, Chandler awoke with a smile. Being in love was great. He rose from the couch and peeked in at Magdalene, who looked like an angel while she slept. They had spent the last three incredible days together, doing nothing out of the ordinary—just enjoying each other in day-to-day life.

Even though they were already married, he decided to do things right and court her, especially since Isabel had said Magdalene had never been courted. When she finally believed he loved her, realized she loved him, and could say the words aloud, then—and only then—would he move into the bedroom.

The dinner bell sounded, indicating the children were awake and ready to celebrate Christmas. Magdalene stumbled out of the bedroom, wrapped in a robe and still looking very much asleep.

"You go. I'll be there shortly." Her eyes were only partially opened.

He kissed the tip of her nose. "You stayed out way too late last night."

She gave him a sleepy grin. "Some handsome fellow and I were spooning on the porch swing."

"Hasn't your father spoken to you about cuddling with

gentleman callers?" He winked. The bell rang again. "The natives are restless." He enfolded her in his arms. "Don't make us wait too long, Mrs. A."

"I won't." She rose on her tiptoes and planted a kiss firmly on his lips.

When he got to the house, the children ran to him. "What took you so long?" Susie asked.

"Were you kissing Miss Maggie *again?*" Bobby's disgusted expression matched the disapproval in his tone.

Chandler ruffled the boy's hair. "Again," he said with a smile.

Bobby shook his head.

"In ten years, you'll be yearning for a Maggie of your own to kiss," Chandler predicted.

Bobby didn't even dignify the remark with an answer.

When Magdalene arrived, she passed out stockings to the boisterous children. Inside, each child found sugarplums, nuts, and candies. "Not before breakfast," she cautioned.

Magdalene had placed a doll for each of the four girls under the tree and a baseball glove for the three boys. They raced to untie the ribbons and unwrap their packages. After smiles, hugs, and thank-yous, Chandler handed the four girls and Magdalene each a box tied shut with a shiny bow. The dresses pleased each lady in his life, but when they wanted to put them on, Magdalene told them, "Not before breakfast."

The boys weren't nearly as excited about their own leather-bound copy of *The Adventures of Tom Sawyer*. "It's one of my favorites, so I wanted you to have your own copy," Chandler informed them.

"One more." Magdalene handed him a shoe-sized box.

Lifting the lid, he found a carved wooden treasure chest. "It's beautiful." He slid his hand over the smooth texture of the wood and admired the craftsmanship. "Thank you so much."

"What's inside?" Sarah asked.

He opened the box. "It's empty." He held it upside down to show the children nothing was inside.

"It's empty so your uncle Chandler can fill it with his own special treasures." Magdalene gazed into his eyes. "Someone is teaching me life is like an empty treasure chest, and we each have to find our own special things to cherish and save." Her expression said she'd found her treasure in him. He wished she'd say those words aloud so they could share the greatest treasure God bestows on a married couple.

He whispered a pointed hint in her ear. "My mother hopes we'll give her at least one grandchild who is ours."

Lowering her lashes, she said, "She does now, does she?"

"Definitely a treasure, wouldn't you say?"

She only smiled and nodded her head.

fifteen

Magdalene kissed Chandler good-bye on New Year's Eve morning. Another week of wedded bliss had passed. She loved this man with her whole heart and was beginning to believe he loved her, so why was he waiting? Some nights, she lay in bed praying he'd come to her—but he never did. She didn't understand why.

Today, his parents had invited all their children and their families for a big dinner and get-together. Chandler went early to meet with his father. They'd been caught up in an ongoing game of chess for almost three weeks now, and both men hoped to play for a few hours this morning before the throngs of people arrived.

Magdalene went into Chandler's office, looking for some postage stamps. She'd written to each of the five boys who had been adopted.

His desk was piled with several neatly stacked papers. A law book on one corner caught her eye, and she wondered what subject he was studying up on. He had the page marked with several pieces of paper. Opening the book, the heading *Annulment laws* jumped off the page. She felt faint. Grabbing the side of Chandler's desk, she lowered herself into his chair. Skimming the page, she read the words Chandler had underlined. *Annul. Different from divorce in that divorce ends a valid marriage. Annulment ends an invalid or illegal marriage.*

Dear God, no! Please don't let this be so. She struggled to breathe—to see. Lifting the papers, she read the top one first.

Dear Mr. Alexandre:
This letter is to inform you as of December 1,
1882, the estate of Warren Baxter will no longer
contribute funds to the San Francisco Christian
Home for Orphans and Foundlings.
Upon Mr. Baxter's death, his nephew now con-
trols the funds and has decided to support other
charities. I'm certain you can appreciate his
desire to use the money here in New York, rather
than sending it out west. We do, however, wish
you success in your venture.

Respectfully,
Winston Wallace Williams III,
Attorney at Law

This letter was the reason Chandler married her in the first place. All her old insecurities reared their ugly heads. *He never loved me—never would have even considered me. . . .* She turned to the second typewritten page.

Dear Mr. Alexandre:
This letter is to inform you as of January 1,
1883, the estate of Warren Baxter will again
be contributing funds to the San Francisco
Christian Home for Orphans and Foundlings.
We will be donating the same amount as before,
so you may continue the work so dear to Mr.
Baxter's heart.

She was no longer necessary in Chandler's life. Queasiness assaulted her, and she covered her mouth with her hand. Tears sprang into her eyes, blurring her vision. She had to blink feverishly in order to finish the letter.

> *Upon reading Mr. Baxter's journals, his nephew, who now controls the funds, discovered the orphanage was his uncle's dearest loved endeavor and most important project. I'm certain you can appreciate his desire to use the money in ways most pleasing to his uncle. We do, however, wish to apologize for any minor problems the young Mr. Baxter may have caused during our brief lapse with the endowment.*

> *Respectfully,*
> *Winston Wallace Williams III,*
> *Attorney at Law*

Shaking, Magdalene placed the third letter at the top of the pile. Written shortly before Christmas, it came from a San Francisco attorney.

> *Dear Mr. and Mrs. Alexandre:*
> *I checked into the current California annulment laws as you requested. From what I discovered, the two of you most certainly do qualify to annul your unconsummated marriage.*

She finally understood. Closing her eyes, she hoped to shut out the intense pain shredding her insides. She laid her head on Chandler's desk. The reason he still slept on the sofa was explained here in black and white. If they truly became man and wife, he could no longer erase their marriage as though it never existed. Lifting her head and wiping her eyes, she finished reading the letter.

> *Since your relationship was built on a need*
> *that no longer exists and since the two of you are*
> *not man and wife in every sense, an annulment*
> *would be relatively simple. Just fill out the*
> *enclosed forms and return them to me with the*
> *fee marked on the fee schedule.*

> *Sincerely,*
> *Jasper Jones, Jr.,*
> *Attorney at Law*

Under the third letter lay the blank forms, just waiting to be filled out.

Magdalene put everything back just the way she'd found it. *God, please get me through the rest of this day.* Tonight she'd sign his forms and return home. She could no longer stay here at the orphanage.

Numbly, Magdalene dressed in her new red dress that Chandler requested she wear. She'd looked forward to having the opportunity to wear it, but now she hated the dress and the deceptive man who'd given it to her. How had he fooled so many people?

Mrs. Lindsay, bless her kind heart, must have sensed something had gone terribly wrong. Never one to ask questions or pry, she did what needed doing. By the time Magdalene finished dressing, that dear woman had all seven children ready to go.

❧

Chandler and his father had sat quietly for a couple of hours, both studying the chessboard, thinking and rethinking each move. Growing restless, Chandler paced while his father scrutinized the previous move.

"Father, can we take a break and talk?"

His father glanced up at him like he'd lost his mind. What sane man would choose conversation over chess?

"Why is it so important to you that I come and work for you? Every time I'm here you bring the subject up."

His father's discomfort showed. He paused a long time before answering. "You've branded me with the reputation of a man who cannot control his own son."

"I meant no harm. I only chose to work at what I love. I have no interest in the shipping business." Chandler returned to his seat across the chessboard from his father.

"You've made me a laughingstock among my friends by choosing to live as a pauper rather than work beside your own family."

"I'm very sorry. I would never intentionally hurt you."

"But you do so every day you continue running that place." His father ran his thumb and forefinger over his mustache.

Chandler had never seen their disagreement from his father's point of view before. "I honestly never intended to cause you pain. I love children and wanted to help them."

"Why not help your own family? What of family loyalty?" When his father's emotions rose, his French accent grew stronger, his English more broken. "Your only loyalty is to Mr. Baxter. He was not your father!" He shook his fist in the air. "I'm your father! The father you never loved or respected."

Taken aback by his father's outburst, Chandler suddenly realized how deeply he'd hurt him. "I did love you—still do love you." He spoke calmly. "But you never loved me. I never measured up to your expectations of a man, was never tall enough, strong enough, or healthy enough." Chandler rose and leaned across the game. "I didn't choose to be sickly as a child."

"I did not blame you. I blamed myself. I had failed to give you good health. With each glimpse at your pale face, I relived the pain of my failure."

Chandler sat back down. His father suddenly looked very old—very old and very lost without Christ. Chandler closed his eyes. *Lord, forgive me for being more of a stumbling block to my father finding You than a light to show him the way.*

"If I come to work for you, you'll forgive me, and we'll start over?" Chandler doubted it, but a part of him hoped.

"If you come to work for me, I will forgive you everything—even the article. And we will start over as father and son. Let's start the New Year on a new step."

Chandler rubbed his forehead, overwhelmed by all that had transpired in his life in just over five weeks. *Lord, what would You have me do?*

"Can you give me time to think and pray and talk to Magdalene?"

He knew because of his father's impatience, he asked a lot. "Little time, but not too much."

"Would you be gracious to Magdalene and treat her as my wife deserves?" He knew he pushed his luck.

"I do not intend to treat her at all."

"That's exactly what I mean. You plan to ignore her, but she's part of our family and worthy of your love and respect. Please, it's most important to me." For her sake, Chandler wasn't above begging.

"I can't understand your fascination with this woman."

His father's perplexed expression made Chandler smile.

"She's the most wonderful human being I've ever met. She makes me want to be more than I am. You and Mother will love her, too, if only you give her a chance."

His father shrugged, clearly thinking only beautiful things were worthy of love. Why was it so hard for the rest of the world to see Magdalene's beauty when Chandler saw it radiate from her?

"Father, there's one more thing: If I come to work for you, I'll still direct the orphanage and probably donate my salary to worthy causes."

"Your news is no surprise." His father moved toward the door. "I'll expect your answer by the end of the week." With those words, he tromped out.

Chandler finally understood his mother's earlier reference, from a couple of weeks ago, to their bad habits; both stayed on the defensive, misreading the other's comments and intentions.

He wondered what Magdalene would say because he felt compelled to take his father's offer. To reach his father with the good news of Jesus, he'd have to enter his world.

ले

Magdalene and the children arrived at the Alexandre mansion precisely at three—just as she'd been told. Oddly enough, nobody was anywhere in sight. She couldn't imagine where all the children were. They usually stayed outside and were as loud as banshees. Everything was uncharacteristically quiet—almost eerie.

Magdalene prayed all the way there, and God's peace settled over her like a protective mantle. He'd get her through this day, and the next, and the next. . . .

Baldwin welcomed them and led the way to the banquet hall.

"Surprise!" Dozens of people shouted in unison. Shocked,

Magdalene glanced around the room at faces she did and didn't know.

Chandler was unexpectedly at her side, kissing her cheek. She forced herself not to flinch. "My mother is throwing a levee for us, Maggie!"

She tried to smile, but her gaping lips wouldn't seem to bend in that direction. Tears pricked her eyes. A party to honor their marriage. What a farce.

Somehow Magdalene mechanically got through the next several hours. First she and Chandler opened gifts—everything a woman needed to run an efficient home. Then they ate dinner. Magdalene forced down the tasteless, cardboard meal, praying it would stay put.

"Now we'll all go out on the back lawn and watch the fireworks display." Mrs. Alexandre spoke the instructions in her polished voice. "I've had the staff set up chairs for everyone. Since we're near the top of the hill, we have a splendid view of the New Year's Eve activities."

"I'm not feeling well," Magdalene whispered to her mother-in-law. "Do you mind if I lie down somewhere?"

"I thought you looked peaked. Does this mean my wish for another grandchild might be coming true?" She was pleased as punch with the idea.

"Mother!" Chandler rebuked her. "Don't embarrass my wife by discussing such personal matters."

She lifted her eyebrows and shook her head. "Please show your lovely bride to the rose room, and Magdalene, I failed to mention how stunning you are in that dress."

"Thank you for all your kindness." Magdalene forced one more smile. "I so appreciate your gesture." And she did. As they climbed the stairs, she considered how hard the woman was working to help her feel welcome and a part of this family.

Given different circumstances, she felt certain they'd grow to be good friends.

Upon reaching the bedroom, Chandler closed the door behind them. "Are you all right?" He attempted to take her into his arms, but she pushed him away and walked to the other side of the room to put some distance between them.

"I needed some postage stamps, but guess what I found on your desk instead?"

He closed his eyes briefly. "Magdalene, it's not what you think."

"You wrote an attorney requesting information about an annulment, and it's not what I think?" She was yelling, but she didn't care.

"You were so unhappy. I didn't know what else to do." His eyes begged her to listen, to understand.

"I know you only married me because of the children, but don't you *dare* pretend you checked into this annulment idea because you were doing me some huge favor. I'm not fooled." Magdalene turned to storm out, but he grabbed her wrist, bringing her to a quick halt.

"What are you saying, Magdalene?" His clenched jaw testified of his growing anger.

"You're the one who wants the annulment so you're free to pursue Isabel. She's the one you wanted to marry in the first place. I only won the honor by default." Sarcasm laced each word.

"Not Isabel again. Are you crazy?"

She tried to pull her wrist free, but he only tightened his grip. "I know the truth, Chandler. I've known since the wedding. I let you talk me out of believing it for a short while, but it's back and glaring me in the face."

"What truth?" He'd never raised his voice at her before.

"You settled for me," she whispered. Magdalene hung her head, hating herself for being unable to get through this confrontation without her tears betraying her deep emotions. Raising her chin, she looked him in the eye. "You loved her. Why didn't you just say so? I gave you every opportunity. You're free. I'll sign the annulment papers tonight."

"Why can't you believe I'm not pining away for Isabel? I know she's your sister, but she's nothing more than a spoiled child. If there were no you, I still wouldn't want to be with her. Please believe me!" His words were raspy.

"Well, there is no me, Chandler, because I'm leaving tonight." She tugged her wrist again, and this time he let go but moved to stand in front of the door.

His eyes misted up slightly. "No matter what I do or say, I can't win your trust. Who hurt you so badly that you let no one near your heart?"

Biting her bottom lip, she wondered if she had the strength to repeat the embarrassing story. She sucked in a large amount of air. "When I was sixteen, a young man named Richard pretended to feel affection for me. No boy had ever noticed me before, so I was quite taken with him. I even allowed him to kiss and caress me, hoping to keep his interest. Turned out, the only part of me he was truly interested in was Gabrielle."

"Magdalene—" His voice carried as much pain as her own did.

"I know I'm not much to look at, but I've recently learned I'm God's treasure."

"And I want you to be my treasure. I'm sorry Richard used you, but I'm not Richard. Must I pay his debts?"

"You can deny you have feelings for Isabel, but I saw the two of you at Woodward's Gardens."

"Talking about your Christmas present!" He ran his hand

through his hair in that familiar gesture she'd come to love.

She stood inches from him, hands on her hips. "I heard it with my own ears!"

"Heard who saying what?"

At least he'd quit denying it. "I overheard Isabel and Josephine—"

Pulling her behind him with a viselike hold on her forearm, Chandler towed her into his mother's sitting room, where Isabel and Josephine giggled over cups of tea. He slammed the door. Both girls startled and gave each other a wary look.

"Isabel, how many times did we meet prior to my marriage to Magdalene?"

Wide-eyed, she answered, "Once."

"When and where?" His clipped words made both girls squirm.

"Here, on Thanksgiving Day." Isabel appeared frightened, and Magdalene felt mortified.

"Did I tell you I loved you or indicate any such emotion?"

Isabel lowered her gaze to her lap. "No."

"Did I ask to call on you or hint at any desire to *ever* see you again?"

Isabel shook her head.

"Josephine, has anything I've said or done given you reason to believe I desired to court, marry, or love Isabel Fairchild?"

"No, Uncle Chandler."

"Then why would either of you girls make my wife believe otherwise, especially on our wedding day?"

Both girls had the decency to look guilty but neither confessed.

"I'm waiting." Chandler tapped his foot, indicating his patience wore thin.

Teary, Josephine looked up. "I repeated a conversation I'd

overheard between my mother and Grandmother."

"I'd like you to repeat it once again for me."

Magdalene bit her lip, not wishing to hear the painful words for a second time.

"Grandmother said you planned to marry so you could claim your inheritance and save the orphanage. The marriage broke Isabel's heart because she'd set her cap for you herself, so I told Isabel you didn't actually love her sister."

"Did you hear me or anyone say that, or did you just assume?"

Josephine hung her head. "I assumed."

Magdalene couldn't keep quiet any longer. "You said Chandler struggled to decide between the two of us, and he ultimately chose me because of my ability with the children."

"I heard Grandmother say—"

"I considered Isabel for about five minutes because she flirted and made me feel like an attractive, interesting man." His face reddened with his words. "Magdalene, on the other hand, kept me at a distance and I wasn't even sure she liked me."

Magdalene recognized the truth of his words and her mistake in treating him with such a detached manner. Her aloof attitude almost pushed him into her sister's arms.

"I want you both to look at me and make no mistake about what I'm going to say." When they did, he continued. "I'm in love with Magdalene—totally and completely. I've never had feelings for another woman, nor will I—ever."

Magdalene's heart reacted to his words by turning a flip in her chest—if only they were true. "Chandler, stop. We don't have to keep up the pretense. I'm tired of all the lies." Her tone was flat, lifeless.

He turned to face her. "I'm tired of pretending too,

Magdalene. I've pretended for weeks that I wasn't in love with you, but I am. I only wanted to save face since you don't share my feelings."

Struggling to believe what she heard, she asked, "Are you saying you love me?"

"I am. I do, and I always will."

She smiled. "You love me? Not the kind of love you have for the orphans, but the way a man loves a woman?"

The door clicked shut, and only she and Chandler remained in the room.

"I love you." His tender expression validated his proclamation. "I don't want an annulment. I never have. Even if you don't love me yet, I don't want you to leave. In case you haven't noticed, I've been working at changing your mind."

"You don't have to work at it. I already do love you, Chandler. I have for the past three years."

He looked puzzled. "Then why—"

"Because I knew you'd never love someone like me—"

"Someone like you?"

"Plain."

"You're beautiful to me. A beautiful woman filled with hidden treasures."

His lips found hers. The kiss was tender, reverent, grateful.

"Let's pack up the kids and go home," she whispered when their lips parted. "I want to be your *wife* before the New Year arrives."

She got no argument from him—only a very happy smile.

epilogue

Thanksgiving Day 1883

Chandler guessed he'd never grow tired of waking up with Magdalene in his arms. Only now, with the huge bulge of their first child protruding from her middle, snuggling her close proved difficult. She stirred and opened her eyes.

"Good morning, Mrs. Alexandre." He kissed the tip of her nose.

A sleepy smile lit her face. "I think this child of ours wants out." Guiding Chandler's hand to her belly, she placed it just so, where he could feel the kicking infant within. The sensation never failed to thrill him.

"We have much to be thankful for." He placed a kiss on her irresistible lips.

She nodded her agreement. "You're at the very top of my list." She touched his cheek.

Turning his head, he kissed her palm. "And you, my beautiful Maggie, are at the top of mine."

"A year ago, I thought I'd be a spinster and never marry."

"And now you're a wife with seven children." He laughed at the irony of the situation.

"Almost eight," she reminded him, patting her tummy. "Funny how life changes."

"I'm glad we adopted them."

"Me, too. Except, now we run an orphanage with no orphans." She laughed.

"For now. I believe God will bring more, but He's giving us time to adjust to our new family and my new job."

"I miss you every day, but I know God changed your heart so you'd be willing to work for your father."

"And Father's, so he'd give me the job and allow us to keep the orphanage open. He's so close to making a decision for Christ." Chandler's words brought excitement. "He asks new questions every day."

Chandler yearned for his whole family to commit their lives to Christ. In the past year, his mother, two of his brothers, and Nadine had done that, but there were so many more. He knew his dad saw the changes in them and hopefully in him, too. Going to work in the family business had been the right thing to do. Chandler felt choked up, thinking about all God had done for and through him in twelve months.

"I have a very special surprise for you today."

"What?" Magdalene's face lit up. She loved surprises.

"Frankie's family and the other four families of the adopted boys are joining us for dinner."

Her eyes misted up. "We'll get to see them all?"

"Every one of them—an orphanage reunion, of sorts."

"I know by their letters they are all happy and well, but to hold them and hug them—how wonderful."

"Frankie is even bringing his puppy! My mother is sending over some of her servants with much of the meal. She didn't want you to have to do a thing but relax."

"Bless that woman! I love your mother."

"And she loves you. Your parents, Gabby, Nathaniel, and their family will be here, too."

"It won't be the same without Izzy." Magdalene's eyes filled with sadness.

"At least she finally sent a letter, and your parents know

she's safe and well."

"I feel so responsible. Once she discovered you loved me, running away must have seemed like the best alternative."

"It was a foolhardy thing to do."

Magdalene turned his head so their gazes met. "I did the same thing. Coming to work here at the orphanage was my way of running from the inevitable."

"But instead, you ran to your future." He kissed her again, but this one was long and slow.

"Maybe Isabel's future is in Arizona."

He loved knowing his kiss caused her to sound breathless. "Maybe." He kissed her again, and she never failed to return his affection twofold. "Maggie, my precious, precious treasure."

They heard at least a dozen feet running down the stairs, resembling a herd of wild elephants. The sound reverberated into their bedroom on the first floor.

"The kids are up." Magdalene giggled. "You're always getting stopped before you get started."

He tweaked her nose. "You should know by now, I don't give up easily."

Their door swung open and seven little bodies piled on their bed. Each one was careful to avoid Mama's tummy.

"Mama, we're awake!" Susie stated the obvious.

"So I see." Magdalene hugged each of them, one by one.

He couldn't have picked a better mother for them or for their baby.

"Will today be the day the baby comes?" Sarah asked.

"I sure hope so. I'd like that, wouldn't you?"

"Yes," all their voices echoed in unison.

Mrs. Lindsay rang the dinner bell. The children raced toward the table. "Walk," Chandler hollered after them.

"Come on, Mrs. A." He rose and gently pulled her up with him. "We have a whole day ahead with nothing to do but be thankful, count our blessings, and sing praise to the Lord."

He wrapped his arms around her expanded girth. "Thank you, God, for my Maggie and all the wonderful treasures You've hidden in her. I am, indeed, a blessed man."

A Letter To Our Readers

Dear Reader:

In order that we might better contribute to your reading enjoyment, we would appreciate your taking a few minutes to respond to the following questions. We welcome your comments and read each form and letter we receive. When completed, please return to the following:

Rebecca Germany, Fiction Editor
Heartsong Presents
PO Box 719
Uhrichsville, Ohio 44683

1. Did you enjoy reading *Hidden Treasures* by Jeri Odell?
   ❏ Very much! I would like to see more books
      by this author!
   ❏ Moderately. I would have enjoyed it more if

   _____

   _____

   _____

2. Are you a member of **Heartsong Presents**? Yes ❏ No ❏
   If no, where did you purchase this book?_____

   _____

3. How would you rate, on a scale from 1 (poor) to 5 (superior), the cover design?_____

4. On a scale from 1 (poor) to 10 (superior), please rate the following elements.

   _____ Heroine   _____ Plot

   _____ Hero   _____ Inspirational theme

   _____ Setting   _____ Secondary characters

5. These characters were special because_____

_____

_____

6. How has this book inspired your life?_____

_____

_____

7. What settings would you like to see covered in future
   Heartsong Presents books?_____

_____

_____

8. What are some inspirational themes you would like to see
   treated in future books?_____

_____

_____

9. Would you be interested in reading other **Heartsong
   Presents** titles?   Yes ❑   No ❑

10. Please check your age range:
    ❑ Under 18   ❑ 18-24   ❑ 25-34
    ❑ 35-45   ❑ 46-55   ❑ Over 55

Name _____

Occupation _____

Address _____

City _____ State _____ Zip _____

Email _____

·····Presents·····